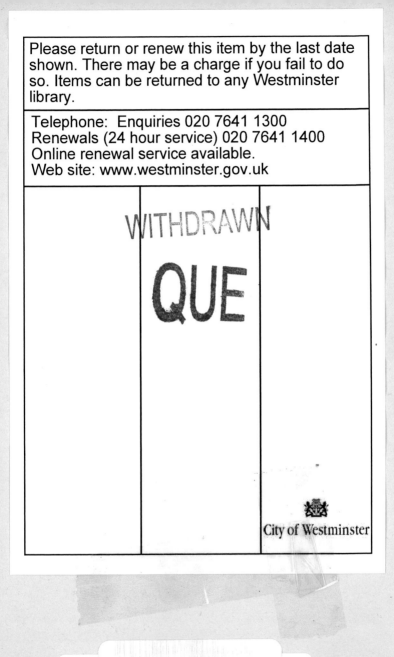

WITHDRAWN

QUE

City of Westminster

Titles in the Tempest Sisters series:
Spring at Taigh Fallon
Jessie's Little Bookshop by the Sea
Summer at Carrick Park
Christmas on the Isle of Skye

Christmas on the Isle of Skye

Kirsty Ferry

Where heroes are like chocolate – irresistible!

Published 2021 by Choc Lit Limited
Penrose House, Crawley Drive, Camberley, Surrey GU15 2AB, UK
www.choc-lit.com

A CIP catalogue record for this book is available
from the British Library

ISBN 978-1-78189-452-1

Printed and bound in Great Britain by Clays Ltd, Elcograf S.p.A.

To my fabulous friends in our extended HCC family.
Love and light to you all.

Acknowledgements

Welcome to Zac and Ivy's story – for readers, who are coming to this very special, and much longer version, of the original eBook novella for the first time, you might want to read *Spring at Taigh Fallon* to learn a little more – well, a lot more – about Angel and Kyle. We touch on the *Taigh Fallon* story in this new version of *Christmas on the Isle of Skye*, but there's much more to the story than I had space for here, and I do hope you will go on and read it – and, obviously, enjoy it!

Zac himself had a semi-starring role in *Spring at Taigh Fallon*, and yes, he's not a Tempest (that honour goes to Rosa, Jessie and Angel in the other *Tempest Sisters* books), but he's Angel's best friend and deserves a happy ending of his own. Or at least that's what lots and lots of people have told me; the readers who fell a little bit in love with the vague, creative, slightly clueless, but very sweet Zac Fallon when they first met him – and the readers who were horrified when Ivy decided to leave Skye and follow her dreams to Glastonbury. I love Glastonbury, and one of my favourite places there is the Chalice Well. I'm fond of telling the story of how I bought a crystal pendulum at the Chalice Well – I was torn between two crystals and chose one. I paid for it, took it out of the shop and it shattered. I went back in, picked the other one up and the lady behind the till nodded knowledgeably and did a straight swap. I had obviously chosen the wrong one first! So, based on that, and the very mystical, magical feeling in that part of the country, I really wanted to set part of this Christmas novel around the Winter Solstice at Glastonbury.

I'm also lucky to have some good friends in the Historical Combat Company – otherwise known as the HCC – who welcomed me with open arms and lots of Pagan hugs when my son first started working towards an Arts Award with them. I've spent some incredible weekends with HCC at Sentry Circle, a wonderful, peaceful campsite in North Yorkshire with its very own stone circle. I witnessed my very first hand-fasting ceremony at the circle and felt very honoured to have been invited to it – and also to be made an honorary member of a particular 'Squad' in HCC – thanks Lily Hannington, Sadie Stewart, Michelle Jones, Kharah Humes, Jill Haswell and Charlotte Paxton for letting me share the mead and the Squad laughs. I know how special the Solstice and Yuletide are to you all, and yours is also a very special "family" to be part of. We've met some incredible people through you – and none more incredible than Gordon Hannington, who we all know was a force of nature and an amazing man. It was an absolute privilege to know him and I'm sure he's still around, keeping watch from Valhalla and the Summerlands.

Thanks must also go to Choc Lit for allowing me to share Zac and Ivy's story, and to the lovely Tasting

Panel who agreed it was good enough to put "out there": Catherine L, Sharon D, Donna M, Allie L, Gill L, Carol D, Hilary B, Cordy S, Maureen W, Yvonne G and Sharon W. I especially loved the comment which said it was "quirky, mystical and heartwarming". The perfect recipe for a festive novel, I reckon. Thanks also must go to my editor who juggled a lot of festive books and still made each one perfect, and also to my cover designer, who excelled herself once again. And thanks, of course, to my family, who, as always during editing time, put up with mutterings, grumblings and very little conversation for a few days. And now it's all done, I can make it up to you and chatter freely again! You are *so* lucky.

And fare thee weel, my only luve!
And fare thee weel a while!
And I will come again, my luve,
Tho'it were ten thousand mile.

From 'A Red, Red Rose' by Robert Burns

Chapter One

The little white-painted house in Broadford that Ivy McFarlane was renting wasn't very big, but it was big enough for her. It was in the centre of the village on the Isle of Skye, and just a short walk away from the café she'd been working at for a couple of months. She'd taken the job as soon as she moved to Skye, but it had only been as maternity cover, and Mary, the girl she was covering for, was due to come back in the New Year.

As Ivy was wandering through the village on her day off, contemplating her options and wondering if she should drop her CV off at a few places, she nipped into the post office to buy some chocolate, certain that a treat would help her to think. Just as she was leaving and tucking the giant family-sized bar securely into her bag, she happened to spot a small handwritten card in the window. Having read the words once, twice, three times, with her heart starting to pound in excitement, she was certain that the card was offering her the most perfect opportunity. She checked nobody was watching, pulled the card off the window and hurried out of the shop, already dialling the number on the advertisement.

As the phone rang at the other end, she promised herself that she'd stick the note back on the window just as soon as possible if she didn't get the job. But Ivy was a great believer in Fate, and was fairly confident she'd be successful – or so she told herself. She was also a great advocate for the power of positive thinking, but it didn't stop her crossing her fingers as the call connected and a soft, distracted Scottish voice answered.

'Hello?'

'Hello?' Ivy paused, wondering briefly what to say to the man at the other end of the phone, and even whether she had dialled the correct number. He hadn't really given her any clues as to who he was in the greeting. 'Ummm – I'm calling about the job advert?' Ivy continued. 'The tea room assistant? At the craft centre?'

'The job? Oh! Oh yes. Sorry. Lots going on here at the minute. Apologies.' There was a sound of banging and what was presumably a workman whistling in the background. 'Let me just leave here so I can hear myself think. That's better. God, I'm sorry. I'm getting work done and it's never-ending.'

'Oh, that's okay. I can call back later if it's more convenient?'

'No, no. It'll never be convenient. Never. So I'm happy to talk now.' Suddenly there seemed to be a smile in the voice, and with it the sense that the speaker was definitely quite chilled and friendly.

Ivy found herself smiling too. 'Good. Like I said, I'm ringing about the job. The tea room assistant. I can basically start in three weeks' time, because my current contract is coming to an end. I've got the relevant experience and it sounds lovely. I mean – a craft centre on the Isle of Skye. It's perfect.'

'It *will* be perfect when the damn place is built. But it's not quite ready yet ...' There was a pause, and Ivy held her breath. 'But you're more than welcome to come and see it as

2

it stands. Where are we now, let's think. Aye. It's the fifteenth. Okay. I'm free on the twenty-first, if that's any good for you?'

'The twenty-first. The Solstice.' Ivy smiled. 'Yes. I can do that. What time?'

'About ten? Do you know where I am – how to get here?'

'Yes. I've got the—I mean I *saw* the advert. I can get there no problem. I just live in Broadford.' She crossed her fingers again. The buses were pretty good; she'd be fine. 'Ten sounds good. Who shall I ask for?'

'Zac. Zac Fallon. I'm easy to find. I'll be the only one here.'

'Great.' Ivy grinned down the phone. 'I'm Ivy McFarlane. I'll see you at ten on the twenty-first.'

If Zac Fallon had thought that business would ease off in December, then he had thought wrong. Also, upon reflection, it probably wasn't the best time of year to be revamping his shop and renovating his house, and there seemed to be no sense of urgency in the contractors he'd engaged to work on the project back in November. Rather, there were cheerful declarations of "we'll be back tomorrow!" and a line of vehicles snaking away down the lane from Zac's premises before the sun began to set – which on the Isle of Skye in December was pretty much before 4 p.m.

On that particular night, the night of the twentieth of December, he raised his hand in farewell as the last vehicle pulled away and turned back to face the building site. His home was an almost-renovated croft, and the almost-renovated-outbuildings next to it were where he made heather gems and polished Cairngorm stones into jewellery. Whilst the outbuildings were being updated, he'd decided to turn one of them into a proper tea room.

3

Currently, he had a few tables and chairs set up in a shed, with an honesty box on the table and some basic tea and coffee making equipment, plus some pre-wrapped snacks he'd bought in for the customers. In the summer months, it was nice to have the tables outdoors, and there was, actually, a pretty steady trade. But he needed to make it a bit more formal, and he hoped that this Ivy girl, who was coming tomorrow for an interview to work in and manage the tea room, would be a good fit for the role.

He strolled into the workshop where his equipment was currently squished in and sat down, meaning to put the final touches to a brooch, when the door flew open and a woman wandered in, dressed from head to toe in black. Her long, raven-coloured hair was carefully curled into loose ringlets and her face was pale. Her eyes were heavily rimmed with kohl, and her lipstick was scarlet. She might have been an imposing sight as she stomped over the flagstoned floor in her chunky biker boots, her long, fitted black coat almost sweeping the ground, but Zac simply looked up and smiled.

'Everything all right, Angel?' he asked.

'Absolutely superb. How are *you*?'

He looked at her suspiciously. 'What? There's something you're going to say – what is it?' He peered over her shoulder, looking hopelessly for reinforcements in the shape of Rosa and Jessie Tempest, Angel's older sisters. He and Angel had met years ago at university and, after one drunken, fumbled attempt at sleeping together in a grotty flat Angel's oldest sister Rosa had briefly lived in, had decided they were better off as friends. It worked much better for them. Angel now had a successful jet jewellery business in Whitby on the North Yorkshire coast, but today she and her sisters were visiting

4

Zac. He had wondered vaguely about how she'd managed to drag them up here so close to Christmas.

It was probably best not to know how, to be honest.

After spending some time with him in the one serviceable public room of his croft, they'd gone off exploring the building site. Zac had thought it best to leave them to it by hiding away in his workshop.

Rosa had always seemed to Zac to be the most sensible of the three Tempests – apart from, in retrospect, the Grotty Flat Era. She now worked at Carrick Park Hotel on the moors near Whitby, and for a long time after the Grotty Flat Incident, Zac hadn't been able to look Rosa in the face – but they were fine now, and he got on well with all three sisters. Being an only child, they'd provided the extended family he'd missed out on, and he felt accepted as part of the family himself.

Jessie – or Jessamine, to give Angel's other sister her full name – owned a second-hand book shop in Staithes, a higgledy-piggledy fishing village a few miles north of Whitby. The three women hadn't scattered too far from their Yorkshire roots at all, really.

Zac was secretly quite glad that the three of them were staying in a hotel this trip; they'd all agreed that the croft was currently appalling, and it just didn't seem as if it would ever be any more than scaffolding surrounding a heap of rubbish at this point.

'I just want to know,' Angel said now, as she stomped towards him and hung over the workspace unhelpfully, 'why you persist with Cairngorm stones. They're from the *east* of Scotland, and you're on the *west*. It's geography, Zachary Fallon. *Geography*.'

'Geography is overrated. Geography really doesn't matter. It's how I fashion the stones that matters.'

'But geography *does* matter actually, because you never come to see me. "Oh no. I won't come to the mainland, Angel – not to the mainland".' Her eyes widened in mock horror, and she slapped her hands against her porcelain cheeks, making a shocked "o" with her mouth. Zac relented and laughed, nodding good-naturedly as he realised the argument wasn't worth pursuing. 'Aye. Not the mainland. You have a point, my Gothic friend.'

Because Zac just didn't particularly like the mainland. He was happy on the Island, only leaving it if he really had to. For instance, on Christmas Eve, he'd be travelling across to the mainland to spend Christmas Day and Boxing Day with his family – but he'd be back after that, and they had promised to come to him for New Year.

'Hmmm.' Angel dropped a friendly kiss on the top of his too-long, messy, light brown hair and he flapped his hand around, waving her out of the way. 'Anyway, are you almost done there? Rosa and Jessie are poking around your tea room to see what's going on and discussing where they'd keep the cakes if they owned it. But I know, I just *know* that it'll be much more pleasant in the hotel lounge. Come on, I'll buy you dinner. We're off in the morning, so we might as well have a nice night.'

'Aye.' Zac put the Cairngorm brooch to one side and stood up. 'I suppose. Anyway.' He walked out from behind the workbench and slung his arm around Angel's shoulder, quietly urging her out of the door before she started inspecting and commenting on all the jewellery in the workshop. 'There's nothing really to see in the tea room at the minute. Just planks of wood. And tools. Many, many tools.' He pulled a face, wondering when the work would actually be complete. It didn't seem as if it would be a quick job at all.

'It's not going to look great for your interviews tomorrow, is it?' Angel commented.

'Interviews!' Zac laughed. 'There's one girl coming through from Broadford.'

'Only one person? Didn't you put an advert out?'

'An advert?' Zac looked at her curiously. 'Well, I made it known that I was looking for someone, and I put a note in the post office window.'

Angel burst out laughing. 'Oh my. People think I'm the one born out of time – I just *look* like I belong in the Victorian age. You *act* like you belong in it. A note in the post office. Oh, I love it.'

'Aye, well. Ivy McFarlane is coming tomorrow, and if she's suitable, I'll take her on. Simple.' He shrugged.

'And if she's not suitable?'

'I'll put another note in the post office window.' He cast a glance down at Angel and winked.

Angel laughed. 'I'm sure Ivy McFarlane will be perfect.'

'Aye. Sure. Which hotel are you in again?'

'You're such a deflection expert. It's the Dunollie. I've told you like a thousand times.'

'Nice.' Zac nodded, thinking of the white hotel on the beach at Broadford. 'I do believe they do a good whisky there.'

'I do believe they do.' Angel ushered him towards her car, and Zac saw two figures coming out of the tea room barn. He lifted his arm and waved. The two fair-haired women waved back in unison and hurried over to him. Whilst Angel was dark-haired and dark-eyed – a look enhanced by her penchant for black clothing – her sisters were the complete opposite. Blonde-haired and blue-eyed, there was no mistaking their family relationship. However, the way the two girls dressed was completely different.

Jessie was almost as unkempt as Zac. The winter winds had whipped her loose hair into something resembling a bird's nest, but she looked delightfully cosy layered into – and she had twanged each layer in turn to demonstrate earlier on – a vest top, a T-shirt and a chunky, white Arran sweater, as well as skinny jeans and padded boots. A sparkly pink pom-pom hat was stuck on the top of her head and a bright pink scarf wrapped around her neck.

Rosa, on the other hand, wore a perfectly cut camel-coloured coat, beige-coloured trousers and brown knee-length boots. She also sported a white scarf and a white cloche hat, with a big white flower on the side. Her hair hung in two perfect plaits, and she looked freezing cold.

'What do you think about my tea room then?' Zac asked them as they approached.

'I hope the kitchen's a reasonable size.' Rosa was a demon in the kitchen and had worked for her godfathers, Donald and Anthony, in their bakery in Whitby before she'd started at the hotel. Zac knew her cakes were out of this world. 'You've got a good space in there, though. Locally sourced and baked stuff would go down a storm.'

'And you should have a kind of library in there,' said Jessie, jabbing her forefinger towards the door. 'Books on the shelves, like a free resource. Take one away, leave one you've loved. Put bookplates in and get people to leave them in other places so you can monitor their travels. How cool would that be?'

'Quite cool,' agreed Zac in his laidback, non-committal way. 'Need to kind of get the barn finished first, though.'

'Of course. But there's nothing wrong with planning ahead,' agreed Jessie, climbing into the back of the car with Rosa. 'I've got *loads* of plans for my shop.'

'You should be careful about over-expansion. Be a bit more sensible,' warned Rosa in that older-sister way she seemed to have, even with Zac. It made him dip his head and smile as Angel rolled her eyes heavenwards and started the engine up. 'You shouldn't run before you can walk.'

'Yeah, yeah. I've been walking a while there though, don't you think.'

The last part of Jessie's sentence hadn't even been a question, and Zac could tell she didn't give a single hoot about over-expansion or being sensible. Books and her bookshop were her absolute passion.

'Have you missed us?' muttered Angel as they drove towards Broadford.

'When are you going back to the mainland again?' he teased.

Angel simply turned towards him and stuck her tongue out.

Ivy's fingers closed around the postcard in her pocket. She'd been carrying it around like a talisman ever since she had "acquired" it from the post office. She had a good feeling about it; she couldn't help it. She was usually quite a positive person and looked forward to whatever the next rung of the ladder was on her career path.

She'd come to Skye with the intention of building her art business, and was already making some good sales in craft shops and galleries around the Island. Coasting her way through art college with top marks, she had loved doing the foundation course that set her on her path, and it had given her a wealth of experience in all sorts of media. Above everything though, she loved lino-printing, and had plans for creating a series based on sites around the Isle of Skye. Maybe more than one series – perhaps Dunvegan Castle, and Portree where the candy-coloured houses overlooked the water. Maybe the Fairy Pools, or the Old Man of Storr ... so much to play with. That could be one series, and the second – well. She didn't know yet, but she had no shortage of inspiration, that was for sure.

Ivy pondered this as she strolled along on a late afternoon walk near the Dunollie Hotel. Although it was quite dark, the windows in the little studios and galleries dotted around glinted with warm yellow and orange lights as the craftspeople finished up for the day. As she walked past the colourful buildings, Ivy glimpsed bright canvases and pretty ceramics, and she yearned to own a little studio like that herself. Sometimes she would simply wander down amongst these small pieces of heaven and daydream of the day she would achieve that – this was one of those "sometimes".

Turning to face the horizon, Ivy stopped and stared up at the Cuillin Mountains, which hung blackly over the Island in the distance, even darker shadows against the velvety, starry winter sky. She shivered with a delicious sense of awe. The Romantics had called these huge landscapes and big skies "sublime", and she could understand where they were coming from.

Just then, her mobile phone rang, making her jump and bringing her back to the present. It was Gideon. She'd met him at art college, and they'd become good friends. Gideon was living and working in Glastonbury now, and it was no secret that it was one of Ivy's many, many creative dreams to do just exactly the same.

'Hey, Gid! Good to hear from you!'

'Hey, Ives. How's things?' His lazy, suspiciously mellow voice made her smile as always.

'Good, good. I'm staring at the most incredible mountains and I've just been on the most incredible beach, and I live in one of the most incredible places in the world. Also, I have a job interview coming up! You?'

Gid chuckled. Even his laughs were laidback. 'And will it be, like, totally the *most* incredible job in the world?'

'Ha! Possibly not, but, *like*, I need a job – and this one has come up. Sooo …' She shrugged her shoulders, even though she knew he couldn't see the gesture. 'Anyway. It's all good.'

'I'll keep my fingers crossed for you. What will it be? Gallery work? I know you'd love that.'

'No. Well – sort of, I suppose. I'd be managing a tea room in a craft centre, so I'm hopeful I'd get to sell a bit of my stuff there too. I'll have to see what it's like.' She touched the card again in her pocket. She'd asked around and memorised the address, and had even done a test trip there on the bus to see what it was like. The place was largely a building site and she hadn't dared go in, but she'd guessed there was a little gem hiding underneath it all, just waiting to be teased out.

'Cool. So, when's the interview?'

'Tomorrow. The twenty-first.'

'The Solstice. Nice one.' Gid had been down in Glastonbury long enough for some of the magic to rub off on

11

him, although he had never really, to Ivy's knowledge, done anything particularly special for the Solstice celebrations, which she thought was entirely odd, especially given where he was living. But that was Gid; he didn't always follow convention, but his intentions to join in were legendary.

'Aye. I've got a good feeling about it, I must say.'

'It's the Solstice vibes, man. They've even reached you up there.'

Ivy laughed and the conversation continued cheerfully as she turned and headed home, past the warm, yellow, welcoming lights of the Dunollie Hotel and the relentless winter waves crashing against the unseen shore behind it, the Cuillins looming mysteriously above it all like some ancient sleeping god.

It was very sublime indeed.

Angel pulled up into the car park of the Dunollie and switched the engine off. The evening was quite dark, although it was barely five o'clock.

'Brrrr.' She shivered exaggeratedly. 'At least the shortest day is tomorrow, so hey – summer's coming. Just as well. The Solstice is a weird, weird time. Have to say, I think I prefer this one to the summer one, though. It's actually moving towards the lighter nights. Not getting darker, kind of thing. Ugh. I for one will be *delighted* to have some lighter nights.'

'Yes. It's about time.' Jessie clambered out of the car. 'I'm really not a winter person.'

'But Christmas is good,' said Rosa. 'I'll give winter that. Christmas is good.'

'Aren't you working it this year? I thought that was why

you couldn't come for Christmas lunch?' cut in Angel. 'And the reason why we're all having it on Boxing Day at the parents' instead.'

'Oh! Well, yes. Of course. We all have to do our bit on the rota, so it'll be a case of me grabbing something to eat from the hotel on the twenty-fifth and having the turkey with you lot on the twenty-sixth. It's fine. It could be worse.'

The sisters continued discussing the arrangements for Christmas as Angel locked up and herded them all into the hotel. The warmth and companionable chatter inside hit Zac as Angel opened the door, and he stood back to let the girls go in first, quietly letting them bicker amongst themselves as to the merits of sprouts or Yorkshire puddings with Christmas dinner.

Angel waved at the receptionist, Rosa peered around the lobby with her polished, professional face on, no doubt comparing it with her beloved Carrick Park, and Jessie ripped off her hat, stamped her boots on the welcome mat and tipped her head upside down to shake her wild bird's nest hair out, pulling her fingers through it in an attempt to tame it. She flipped her head upwards again, and the blonde mane stood out around her head like a dandelion clock as she narrowed her eyes and looked around for, Zac assumed, any abandoned books on the tables.

As the Tempest sisters finally got inside the place, he looked along the street and a figure caught his eye. It was a girl, walking towards the hotel, laughing at something someone was saying on the phone she had pressed against her ear. A car drove past and illuminated her in the headlights, and he found he couldn't stop staring at her. She had fair hair, pulled back in a messy bun, and she strode along in bright red wellingtons. She wore a blue coat and dark blue jeans, and had the brightest smile he'd seen in a long time.

The car drove past, and the muted lights of the hotel windows caught her as she walked away into the distance and disappeared into the shadows. Zac had the oddest sense of recognition. He shivered and looked up at the Cuillins. They seemed to be holding a secret inside of them, just watching him; simply waiting, biding their time.

He became aware of the waves crashing onto the nearby shore, and he shivered again.

'You coming in for that whisky, Zachary Fallon?' called Angel, beckoning him in furiously.

'Aye. Sure.' He looked again to where the girl had been, but the darkness had swallowed her up.

Aye. The Solstice, and the days leading up to it, had a very strange magic about them indeed – even he could feel that.

So, he turned back to the hotel and hurried indoors, grateful for the warmth of his friends waiting inside for him.

Chapter Two

The next day, Ivy alighted from the bus and walked the short distance into the large car park whilst a light flurry of wet snow fell on her shoulders. In front of her, she saw a couple of long, low barns that were swarming with workmen. Again. One of the barns had some tables and chairs stacked up outside, so she assumed that was the one ear-marked to be the tea room.

She recalled she had said that she'd be available to work there in a couple of weeks – but it didn't even look like the place would be finished by then. But who knew? She had no knowledge of construction, and perhaps these cheerful looking men would perform miracles.

She turned and saw a house a little further along, which was also covered with scaffolding, but beneath that, she could see a sympathetic new-build emerging from the existing croft. It would be stunning when it was done – but again, it didn't look as if it would be finished any time soon either.

A man came around the corner of the croft. He was tall, slim and slightly dishevelled, and as he came closer, she saw that he was frowning. His mousey-brown hair was flopping over his forehead and reached down almost to his chin. It didn't look like a thought-out, designer-stubble sort of look – just a rather handsome, distracted man who probably wasn't aware just how handsome he was. He looked up as she was studying him, and she felt her cheeks heat up as he focused on her, seeming to start a little.

He smiled a little warily. 'Ivy? Ivy McFarlane?'

'Yes! That's right. You must be Zac.'

'I am, aye.' His smile grew wider and he looked at her almost curiously. Then he nodded across to the workmen. 'I may have lied when I said I was the only one here. As you can see, there are other people here, but I'm the only one who's not a workman. So I'm kind of correct, I think.'

'Kind of.' Ivy laughed. 'Look, if it's not convenient I can come back. Just like the phone call.' She waved her hand in the direction of the building site. 'I guess you won't be ready to employ anyone for a while anyway.'

'Well, they tell me it'll be done by New Year, but I'm not certain I believe them.' He pulled a face and indicated the barn with the tables outside of it. 'You can get in. It's quite safe, apparently, but I promise it'll be a lot nicer when you come to work here. Let's go and have a look at it.'

When she came to work here? But she hadn't even had the interview yet! Perhaps that was a good sign? Or maybe he was just as vague as he looked and hadn't realised what he'd said. *Not to worry.*

She didn't say anything, just followed him as he began to walk over to the barn, talking to her about his plans.

'So, yes, that's going to be the tea room. We get a lot of passing trade from people leaving Armadale, where the Mallaig ferry drops them off. And like it said in the advert, there's a gift shop too.' He looked uncomfortable. 'It all sounds a bit corporate and hard-hearted, doesn't it?'

Ivy hid a smile. 'Not at all. You've got a business to run, and people love things like that.'

'True.' Zac nodded thoughtfully. 'I make jewellery in *that* barn – we can go in there in a minute. I'm afraid that you'll not get much out of me if I'm working, though. Which is another good reason I need someone managing the tea room. Someone who can actually be nice to visitors without scaring them off. Also, I function better when I've got caffeine at hand. I really need to learn not to drink all the profits from the tea room,' he mused, frowning again. 'Anyway. Aye. I make jewellery.' He shrugged and opened the door, gesturing that Ivy should go in before him.

'So, you sell your jewellery in the gift shop, yes? I make jewellery too – but I'm more of an artist than a jeweller, if I'm honest. I work with crystals a lot, though. And I love doing lino prints. I think that's my favourite sort of art. In fact, that's one of the reasons I decided to come to Skye … for the inspiration, I guess.'

'And is it working so far?' asked Zac.

'Oh, aye! But to be honest, I'm just renting in Broadford. I didn't want to commit to living here properly, but I wanted to experience it. I did a work placement at Glastonbury when I was a student, and it was absolutely magical. I loved every minute. I'm really excited to be on Skye, but I still think I need to go back to Glastonbury at some point. I've got good memories of the place. And I *will* go at some point. I will indeed. But not for a while. Don't worry.' She flashed him the widest, most guileless smile she could muster – realising too late that it maybe wasn't the best thing she could say to a potential employer.

Zac, however, didn't seem to notice.

Instead, he nodded. 'It's good to have a plan. But you know, in the meantime, if you want some space on the shelves, it's yours.'

'What? Really? Oh, that's great. Thank you.' *The smile must have worked.*

'Good. So, what do you think about the tea room then?'

They stood in the building and Ivy could genuinely imagine what it would be like with everything in its place. She told him about the café she currently worked in, and what the layout in there was and soon, in her mind, this place was kitted out and ready to receive visitors.

After that, Zac took her into the other barn and gave her a tour of the workspace. It all looked wonderful. He showed her his work in progress, and they chatted about all the different aspects of jewellery making.

And finally, they walked out of that barn and headed to the middle of the car park. The snow flurries had stopped but it was still pretty cold, and she pushed her hands in the pockets of her blue coat. She guessed he'd take her somewhere to start the proper interview now.

'Oh. And the croft,' he said, instead of something more interview-like, such as "please may I see your CV". 'That's going to be done last of all. I can put up with it a bit longer in there, so long as they get this lot sorted first. It's just me, like I say. I can hide out in one room if I have to.'

'Or sleep in the barn.'

'Or sleep in the barn. Aye. Or I've got that derelict croft over yonder on my land.' He nodded over to a ruin at the far end of the site. 'No roof, though. Bit of a damp problem. Maybe not a great idea, eh?' He turned to face her and looked down at her, smiling. 'So. When did you say you could start then? Just after New Year would be good for me.'

Ivy was taken aback and blinked. 'Oh. Aye. I should be okay for just after New Year. But don't you want to, like, interview me properly? Or something?'

Zac shrugged. 'Or something. Nope. I'm not going to

bother with any more interviews. You seem like you'll be perfect. Anyway, you're the only one who applied soooo ...'

'Ha!' Ivy thought it prudent not to mention the now crumpled piece of card in her pocket. 'Well. If you're happy to have me, I'm happy to work for you.' She smiled back up at him, and they shook hands.

A strange little tremor ran up her arm as their hands connected and their eyes met. Ivy blinked, and she was aware that they held that gaze between them for longer than probably necessary.

'Great,' she said, feeling a little thrown. 'I ... I look forward to it.'

'Me too,' he responded. 'It'll be good to get to know you. One thing—' Here it came – he was going to have to reduce the salary, or there was some other catch that would make this opportunity much less perfect than it had first seemed ...

'Aye?'

'Were you in the village yesterday evening – walking along by the Dunollie?'

'Indeed I was.' Ivy was curious. 'Did you see me? Actually. Silly question. Of course you saw me – otherwise why would you be asking that.'

Zac's lips turned up in a lovely, slow, lopsided smile and his dark eyes crinkled a little at the corners. 'Aye. I saw you. You were on the phone.'

She waited for a moment, then realised that she wasn't going to get much more out of him.

That sweet vagueness was a trait of Zac's she was to see much more of over the coming months.

Chapter Three

The Isle of Skye, January

The workmen had, surprisingly, finished the work on schedule, and Zac's craft centre and tea room were open again fully by the first week in January. Ivy was installed there by the second week in January, and so far, so good. She was happy, he was happy and the customers loved it.

Zac had a little core of regulars; walkers and families mainly, who frequently came out there to enjoy the refreshments he had always provided. Being open in those grey and gloomy days in early January, after the excitement of Christmas had waned and everyone was yearning for some sort of routine and for food that was not beige and snacky, had paid dividends. Ivy had been providing cakes and scones and quiches and soups, and had rapidly proved herself indispensable. She was cheerful and welcoming and exactly what visitors wanted to see on a cold, wintry day.

Zac had found also that his gift shop was doing splendidly. Ivy had brought some of her items through to pop on the shelves, and she was almost ready to restock. So, it was with a cheerful air that Zac wandered into the tea room as Ivy was closing up one night and responded to her open, friendly smile with one of his own.

'Nearly done,' Ivy said, wiping the counter down and tidying up the last few things.

'Good,' replied Zac. 'Because it's a Saturday night, it's my birthday and we're going to celebrate. We've both got the day off tomorrow, so I've decided.'

'Thank you very much for the unexpected day off – but your *birthday*!' Ivy glowered at him. 'You never said! How old?'

'Twenty-nine.' He pulled a face. 'I know, I look older.'

'No, you don't! Happy birthday.'

'Thank you.' He inclined his head politely and shoved his hands in his pockets. 'I thought we could go to a ceilidh. There's one on at the local. If you fancy it. They have a fine selection of whisky as well.'

'Ooh, I'm sold.'

'Excellent. I'll give you a lift home, then come back and collect you about seven?'

'Are you sure?'

'What about? Giving you a lift home or coming back to collect you? Both. I'm sure about both.'

'All right. I've never been to a ceilidh. Will it be fun?'

Zac grinned. 'It depends on your definition of fun,' he said, and couldn't help but wink at her.

It was lovely to see her face light up as she laughed.

The ceilidh was absolutely exhilarating – it was even better and even more fun than Ivy could have anticipated.

From the moment she'd walked in, escorted on Zac's arm, the warmth and vigour of the pub hit her.

'I have to say, I've been in here before – but I've never seen it buzzing like this!' She stared around her, feeling the smile tugging at her lips as she saw the groups of people clustered around, already enjoying drinks as the live band played some traditional folk tunes to warm the place up.

'Aye. It's a sight to see,' replied Zac, guiding her to a table. 'I'll get the drinks in. I recommend at least one whisky to give you the confidence to dance. Angel is embarrassing at these things. I hope you don't start crying at the "Skye Boat Song".'

Zac had told her all about Angel and her quirks, and Ivy smiled at the image. 'I'm made of tougher stuff than that,' she teased, and sat back as Zac was swallowed up into the crowd at the bar.

After that first whisky, the evening started to go a little fuzzy at the edges. But she knew she enjoyed herself immensely.

At one point, the chap leading the ceilidh called out a Hooligan's Jig, and Ivy stared up at a merry Zac in surprise. 'What the heck is that?'

'Ah! It's this!' He laughed, and his arms fastened around her waist, and soon it felt as if she was spinning around like a top as the fast music pounded out and couples went crazy. They were whirling around, swapping dance partners and laughing hysterically as people threw themselves into the largely un-coordinated dancing.

Other couples whooshed past her as Zac's arms were once again around her waist, whirling her around. She threw her head back and laughed, and when he set her back on her feet, the room kept spinning and she stumbled. He lunged and caught her by the elbow, setting her upright. As he did, his face came very, very close to hers, and there was suddenly the oddest look in his eyes – something between humour and concern and sheer joy …

It made her heart skip even more beats and made her feel dizzier than ever. Coupled with the warmth of his hands through the cotton fabric of her blouse, she didn't know if she was coming or going for quite a few moments after she'd landed.

Eventually, at the end of the evening, they stood outside the pub, arms around one another companionably, talking absolute rubbish to each other. He kissed her on the cheek briefly as she got into her taxi and told her he would wait for his own. His car, apparently, would spend the evening in the pub car park, to be retrieved the next day when the whisky had worn off.

Ivy got home and promptly got into bed, reliving that dance and that little kiss over and over and over until she fell asleep.

In the morning, it all just seemed like a big, wonderful dream.

It seemed even more of a dream when she rocked back up at work on Monday morning, and Zac was the same as ever towards her; friendly, a little vague and very lovely.

He didn't say a lot, did Zac. She was learning that gradually.

But the night of her first ceilidh and that little kiss on the cheek was yet another dream she felt she would always be reluctant to let go.

Chapter Four

The Isle of Skye, April

As the weeks wore on, Zac and Ivy settled into an easy friendship and a good working relationship. It seemed as if all was going well, until Zac received a stiff, official-looking letter from some solicitors.

As he opened it and read it, and read it again, he frowned. He didn't quite know what to make of how he felt. The letter told him that, with deepest regret, his Great Aunt Jeanie had died. Reading further, he found himself a most unwilling beneficiary in her will. So, the first thing he did, when he found out he had inherited Jeanie's big old Highlands house, Taigh Fallon, was to make a panicked phone call to Angel. He couldn't dump this on Ivy, no matter how friendly they'd become over the last couple of months. It wasn't exactly professional, was it? Running to his staff with such a Pandora's box of information.

No. Angel was definitely the person he needed to speak to – it wasn't every day you discovered you'd suddenly been lumbered with an old-lady house on the shores of a loch on – heaven forfend – the mainland. So, he rang his best friend; the person who would understand *exactly* how he felt.

'Angel?' His voice sounded unsteady even to him.

'Are you all right? You sound a bit … weird.' He imagined the concern in her pretty face as she answered him.

'No. I'm not all right … I've just inherited a house.'

'A *house*? Who from?'

'My great aunt.'

'Is that the one who used to come and see you? Oh Zac, I'm so sorry.'

'Yes. Jeanie. She'd always come to us, really. I haven't been to her house since I was little. I remember one time I went, she was all dressed in black like Poe's raven – no offence.' He pushed his too-long hair off his face and scowled into the phone. He could say some stupid things sometimes.

'No offence taken. But seriously?'

'Seriously.' Zac pushed the papers around his desk, not knowing what else to do with them. 'As I grew older, I got to know her better, and she was so lovely. We used to meet up with some other family members at her house when I was very young, but they lived abroad and didn't come home very often. I remember playing with an older cousin. He was called Kyle ... he was a bit of a pain.' He scowled again, remembering the older boy. 'He thought he was ten times better than me because he was older, and I thought he had a loud voice and a weird accent. He tore the head off my Action Man once. And he wouldn't let me read any of the good books Aunt Jeanie had. Told me I was too little and put them on a shelf out of my reach.' There was a shocked gasp from Angel, which was gratifying to hear, and he pressed on, offloading to her. 'Anyway, I just got this letter and it's talking about some old, convoluted inheritance thing where the house gets divided between the members of the youngest generation.' He rustled the papers more furiously and compressed his lips to try and stop himself rambling on.

But he couldn't stop himself for long, because the whole situation was just ridiculous and unnecessary. What on earth did he need a house on the mainland for? 'Which means I get some, and if they find anyone else, they'll get a share too. I can't quite believe that she wanted somebody like me to have the place!'

Angel seemed to find that amusing. He heard the smile in her voice as she responded, 'If they find anyone else? You mean like a random relative they dredge up? Or maybe that cousin you mention. Who sounds vile, by the way.'

'Aye. Mam thinks they're still in Canada. All she ever heard was family hearsay, though.'

'As if anyone from Canada is going to be interested in an old-lady house.' There was a slight pause, then she came back on. 'Look. I've got to go, I've got some customers. I'll call you later, okay?' Of course – she was at work, and he was totally dumping all this on her. How thoughtless of him. He immediately felt guilty,

'Okay. Talk later.'

'Bye for now.'

'Bye, hen!' Zac disconnected the call. *Hen*. He'd called her *hen*? Clearly, he was truly distracted. He hadn't called Angel "hen" ever. He hardly ever called anyone "hen". He had to be completely discombobulated to do that.

And he was.

Ivy was absolutely loving the craft centre and tea room, and knew she had done absolutely the right thing by pilfering that card from the post office. She had never ever been so happy in a job. She was loving working in the tea room, loving working with crystals and especially loving working with lino prints. She had discovered that the beautiful, mysterious Isle of Skye spoke to her like no other place on earth –

except maybe Glastonbury, which still bubbled around her consciousness with a pull that she couldn't quite describe.

But here on Skye, Glastonbury seemed like a million miles away, and she fully understood that visitors to the Island were either highly excited to be on Skye, or sad they were leaving, so they wanted souvenirs. Zac had been right, of course, to provide a gift shop, and it hadn't been long before Ivy's work was also on display and selling well. Zac had been very impressed with it, and she already had some ideas for a new series of prints. Limited edition, maybe.

And after much debate with herself, she'd also given Zac three small crystals to show him the sort of thing she was working with, and he'd had them clustered on his workbench ever since. They were very lovely indeed, even if she said so herself. Although, she wasn't quite ready to let him know what each one symbolised …

But, with the experience she'd had working in cafés and tea rooms, her cakes and treats were also out of this world, and they were all helping Zac's business to take off. He'd told her he still needed to work on building the business up, hinting that he'd like her on board to do that, and she was super excited to be part of it all. Life was good and she was very happy indeed on Skye.

On this particular day, a fresh batch of cheese scones was just out of the oven, and Ivy had put a new pot of coffee on to brew. The mingled scents were divine. Tying her hair back more securely, she sniffed surreptitiously, ear-marking one of the scones for her tea break. In fact, she suspected Zac would be partial to one of those scones as well, and put one on a plate for him, alongside hers, with a pat of golden, creamy Skye butter. She knew too well what he was like – and somehow felt it her duty to ensure he was fed and watered throughout the day. Which was ridiculous, because he was a grown man and well-used to looking after himself, remote as he was up here.

'Don't you ever get lonely?' she'd asked him once as they sat on a wall with a coffee after an exceptionally busy day.

He'd looked at her curiously, that funny, lopsided smile he had lifting the corners of his lips, little crinkles showing briefly at the side of his eyes. 'Lonely, lassie? Of course not. I have everything I need right here.'

'But your family – aren't they on the mainland?'

'Aye.' He'd nodded slowly. 'But it's not a million miles away, is it? And they like to visit, so …'

'So … you don't ever go over to see them?'

'Oh, I do. I just don't stay there.' He grinned at her, teasing. 'I went to the mainland last Christmas, didn't I? And I have plenty of friends on the Island, which is perfect.'

'But you live so far away from them all.'

'Not really. I know where they are if I need them, and they know where I am.' He shrugged and looked down at her. 'And some are closer than others.' He'd looked away quickly after that, and pointed out some random bird that she'd agreed looked very majestic indeed.

But his words had echoed curiously around her head all night after that, and she had wondered if she was reading too much into it all.

But today, the most important thing was getting those glorious scones separated from the rest of the batch. And eating them. Of course.

Ivy checked the tea room, noticing that everyone seemed happy and contented, and nipped outside. There were no cars pulling into the car park, so she scurried along to the workshop with a scone and a coffee, intending to deposit them with Zac while she had the chance.

As she got to the door and peeked in, Zac was scrolling furiously on his phone, the piece of jewellery he'd been working on apparently abandoned as he scowled at the screen.

'Cheese scone?' She smiled as Zac looked up, transferring his scowl to her. 'And a coffee? Or is your phone more interesting? And stop scowling at me.'

'Scowling?' Immediately, he looked contrite. 'Sorry. I've just – well – inherited a house.'

'You've just *what*?' She almost dropped the plate on the table, and there was definitely some slopping of the coffee as she set the mug down beside it. 'Inherited a *house*?'

He glanced quickly up at her and raised his eyebrows. 'You just answered your own question. But yes. I inherited a house.' He waved the phone at her. 'Here. Here it is. My Aunt Jeanie's place. She ... died.'

'I'm so sorry to hear about your aunt. Did she live here? On Skye?' The thought whizzed into her head and out again. She was fairly sure he hadn't mentioned an Aunt Jeanie who lived on the Island, but you never knew. She herself had "aunties" and "uncles" who weren't related by blood, but were close friends of the family. Perhaps he'd looked after some little old lady on the Island who had struggled through the sometimes harsh winters, and she'd left a cottage to him?

'Thank you. But no. No ... I wish she did. This place – it's ... it's ... on the *mainland*.' He looked up at her again, something like horror in his eyes. 'Look. Right here. On Google Maps.'

His face was so outraged and panicked that Ivy, to her shame, bit her lip to stop herself from laughing at his expression. 'Let me see.' She came around the worktable and bent over the phone. She could see what looked like a nineteenth-century manor house set in large gardens right next to a body of water. 'Zoom out, would you?' she asked, and he obliged. The body of water turned into a loch, and right on the far side of the loch, she could see the familiar outline of Eilean Donan castle. 'Oh my, that's beautiful!'

'I haven't been to Taigh Fallon since I was a bairn – I'd completely forgotten what it looked like. Jeanie liked to travel, and we tended to see her in passing when she was stopping off on her jaunts here, there and everywhere.' Zac stared at the picture on the phone and shook his head. 'I can't believe she's gone … and I can't believe she's done this.'

'She must have loved you a lot. What are you going to do?'

'I'd sell it. But it's not up to me. I haven't got one hundred per cent of a say in the matter.'

'Why not?'

'Because there is a chance a random Canadian cousin will turn up. I haven't seen *him* for years either. But it seems it's to be shared between us.'

'Wow.' Ivy was, for once, speechless. It wasn't the sort of thing you expected to learn when you delivered cheese scones to the boss. 'If you need to go and sort things out, I'm happy to look after this place for you?'

'Thanks, Ivy. That's appreciated. Hopefully, it won't come to that. I mean – the *mainland*!' He pulled a face again. 'Best case scenario is my cousin says "forget it", and wants nothing to do with the place. Then we can just agree to sell it. Get rid.' He looked out of his window at the Cuillin Mountains looming up across the moors, and his mouth turned down at the corners. *Poor guy*, thought Ivy – he'd just lost a relative and gained something he didn't want in the process.

Ivy longed to give him a hug, but she settled for squeezing his shoulder instead. She had a feeling that whatever he decided, he'd not be leaving Skye to relocate.

Weirdly, that made her feel better.

She put it down to the fact that she loved her job.

Later on that evening, when the craft centre was all locked up and he was trying to relax in his perfectly renovated croft (he realised now that the workmen had been true miracle workers), the irrepressible Angel texted Zac to let him know that, if he wanted to continue the conversation, she was home from work, and he immediately called her back – he'd never been so glad to speak to her.

'Zachary Fallon! Or must I call you "Sir", now you've inherited property?' Her voice was cheerful, and he could hear a kettle bubbling to the boil somewhere close to her. He imagined her in Whitby, settling down in the tiny lounge of her little fisherman's cottage, affectionately nicknamed Goth Cottage, with her black – of course – coffee, putting her feet up on the sofa to let him offload yet again.

Zac grunted in disagreement at the thought of anyone calling him "Sir" and picked up where he'd left off. They'd known each other for so long, and knew each other so well, that he didn't need to recap anything. He knew Angel would remember exactly where they'd ended one conversation, ready to start another. 'I've Google-mapped it,' he said, "it" being Taigh Fallon and thus needing no further explanation. 'It's definitely on the mainland, and … it's not an old-lady house. It's bigger than I remember it; it's truly a mansion thing, Ange.' He pronounced it "Aynge".

'A mansion thing?' Angel sounded intrigued.

'Yes. It's in the Western Highlands, near Loch Long and the Falls of Glomach – I think it's near Eilean Donan castle.'

'I love Eilean Donan. Very atmospheric.'

'Yes, yes. And you hate Glencoe because you reckon it's still haunted with memories of the massacre hundreds of years ago. I know all of that. Ange – what I don't know, is what I should *do*. They've even sent me a key! This big old iron thing that looks as if it should unlock a mausoleum.'

Mausoleum. He realised too late that this was probably the wrong thing to mention to Angel, if he wanted her to agree that selling the place was the best thing to do.

He closed his eyes in despair as she verbalised the very thing he knew he *should* do, but really didn't want to do.

'Go there,' she said simply. 'Go and see what it's like properly, with you being an adult now and all that.'

'But I don't *want* to go there. I've got more than enough going on here to see to.' He glared at the key and the letter, spread out on his coffee table in front of him. He had loved Aunt Jeanie, and thought she would have known him well enough to realise that owning a property on the mainland – especially a property the size of Taigh Fallon – was something that was simply not in his game plan.

'You sound like a spoilt brat, Zac. Can't Ivy manage for a week or so?'

Okay, now he felt *exactly* like a spoilt brat, and flushed as he remembered Ivy's offer to look after the place for a little while if he needed her to. In desperation, he tried one more deflection. 'Why should she? It's *my* business.'

'And I'm sure she's more than capable of selling cakes and making coffee and showing people your beautiful jewellery. Look, it's April, I know you're busy, but there are bound to be bitey insects on Skye. There always is, in my experience. Escape them – go to the old-lady house!'

'The midges aren't confined to Skye, you know? They'll be on the mainland too.'

'You should still go.' There was an ominous silence, and Zac suddenly knew what was going through his best friend's head. And yes. Here it came. 'I'll come with you, if you like.'

There was a brief pause as he stared at the phone. In one way, that would be perfect – but in another, it could well be a disaster. One sniff of an old property, and Angel always fell head over heels in love with it, her mind becoming full of romantic, Brontë-like notions. 'You'd come?' asked Zac. He knew he didn't sound the most grateful person in receipt of such a generous offer, but this *was* Angel.

'Yes. I guess I would.' There was a smile in her voice. He was one hundred per cent sure it was a self-satisfied smile as well.

Okay – one more weapon in his arsenal. 'But who'll look after your workshop?'

'The workshop can look after itself. I suspect Grace Nelson would like to run it, but as she's only six, I think I'll just lock it up for a week.' Grace was a little girl whose father owned the photographers opposite Angel's Whitby workshop, and who often wandered in to assist Angel, whether she wanted the assistance or not. Despite the situation, Zac couldn't help but smile at the idea, and Angel continued. *Smugly*, he thought. She continued quite smugly. 'No harm done. It's not really peak holiday season yet, and Whitby Goth Weekend is at the end of the month, so we're fine. Jessie might pop in to check it over if I ask her, but I'm not bothered.' Zac knew that Jessie wouldn't have a problem with that – it was something she often did, as she had a few contacts in Whitby and was in the habit of collecting books from her suppliers every couple of weeks anyway. Zac swore that half of the books never made their way into Jessie's shop. Once, he'd been visiting Angel on one of his rare trips to Whitby, and Jessie had come into the jet workshop looking terribly furtive, hugging a box to her chest as if it held the crown jewels. 'Jessie was just here three days ago for books,' Angel had informed him. 'She said she still had some gaps on her shelves and needed to fill them. I pointed out that shelves at home are quite different—'

'Silence!' Jessie had hissed, her eyes darting to and fro. 'I never said *where* I was going to put them.' Zac had assumed (correctly, Angel had told him later), that the books were largely destined for Jessie's own cottage, to pile up on the shelves she had lining the attic.

Rosa and Jessie definitely felt like sisters to him as well. It was weird, though – whenever he let himself think of Ivy, she never felt like a fourth "sister", despite the fact they'd got on so well from the first moment they met.

With Ivy, things just felt … different. It was this he was musing on, when he realised Angel was probably waiting for an answer.

He blinked and brought himself back to the present, realising the thought of Ivy had distracted him from the main issue here. 'You think I should go then?' He knew he sounded pathetic and wished Angel was here in person to give him a slap or something, to shake him out of it.

'For goodness sake!' Angel sounded exasperated, and

that was good – that was exactly the sentiment he needed to hear. He smiled down the phone, knowing it was pointless to respond because she clearly hadn't finished. 'Yes! Look – give me the weekend, then I'll set off Sunday evening.' Aye. She had answered her own question – *just like Ivy had earlier*, he thought, then quickly dismissed the thought, concentrating on Angel again. 'I'll stop off in Edinburgh and come up to Skye on Monday. Or I can meet you at the old-lady house. It's up to you.'

'Come to Skye first.' Okay, he was suddenly relieved that Angel was coming. He really did need to sort this out, and she was the perfect person to do it with – *well, maybe not as perfect as Ivy*, his subconscious muttered, but he quashed that thought, as it was bloody ridiculous to assume Ivy would even be up for that. And anyway – it was ages since he'd seen Angel and he had lots to show her. The bloody renovations were complete for a start, *hallelujah*! 'You can see what I've done to the place since last time.'

'No problem. You sure you're okay with this before I come? You'll not decide to hole up in your croft and not bother?'

Zac sighed. Chance would be a fine thing … *but holing up with Ivy at the croft?* … he shook the thought away. It was completely the wrong time to be thinking that. 'No, you're right. It needs to be done. I owe it to the old girl, I suppose. But I don't want to be staying there overnight. I don't like the mainland.' *A day* – he'd give himself a day. That would be long enough.

'You do owe it to Jeanie to go. And you are very silly about the mainland. We don't all bite, you know? Not as much as your horrid island midges do, anyway. Right, I'm going to sort my packing out. I'll see you Monday, and I'll have my usual room, yes? You haven't messed *that* one up too much with your renovations, have you?'

'Of course not. And anyway, it's far too pokey for a normal human being to sleep in. I can't do anything sensible with it. See you Monday. And thanks.' He always teased her with the fact that "her" room was approximately the size of a coffin, and therefore suited her perfectly.

'I'm only coming because I'm nosey.' He could hear the smile in her voice again.

'I know.' He hoped she heard the answering smile in his.

Ivy's heart was beating far too fast. She had just had a call from Gideon, and she desperately needed to speak to Zac. A chance had, *finally*, come up for her to go down to Glastonbury, and it wasn't something she needed his permission for – not at all – but she wanted to see his face when she mentioned it. Just in case.

'Hey, Ives,' Gid had said, his voice warm, cheerful and suspiciously mellow yet again. 'Might be a studio space coming up down here for you, babes. Not until the summer, though. But have you got any thoughts? Like, immediate thoughts? Like right now thoughts?' He'd chuckled, but Ivy knew he was serious. Studio spaces down there were like gold-dust.

There was one fly in the ointment though, she'd gradually come to realise; the mystical, beautiful and steeped-in-folklore Glastonbury was in Somerset, at the bottom end of England. It was almost as far away from Skye as she could possibly get. If Gid had asked her that question a few months ago, she wouldn't have given it a second thought. A rental car would have been packed, she'd bunk with Gid until she found a place, and she'd be off like a shot, living her best life.

But now – now, something stopped her from agreeing on the spot and high-tailing it down there. That something was a job she loved, a place she loved … and, she realised suddenly, Zac.

The realisation that she cared a great deal about Zac had stolen across her over the few months they'd worked together, and Zac was now so much a part of her that she found it difficult to separate her feelings for him from a job and a life she adored.

But, when she thought about it, he'd never given her any *real* indication that he felt the same way.

So, this was why she needed to see his face. God knew that his words wouldn't tell her what she wanted to hear, but she thought she might be able to read his face when she told him.

Ivy took a deep breath and knocked on the door of Zac's croft. It took a moment for him to open it, and he seemed to do a double-take when he saw her. His eyes widened and he held his hand out, before quickly withdrawing it again. 'Ivy! What's up? Have you left something at work?' He turned away, presumably reaching for the keys to the public buildings, which he kept on a big hook just behind the door.

'No! No – I haven't left anything. I – I just wanted to talk to you about something.' She felt her face tense into a frown and made the effort to smooth her expression out again. Zac looked at her curiously, his hand hovering uncertainly.

Eventually, he dropped his hand to his side and pulled the door wider. 'Do you want to come in? Sorry, I've got stuff all over the coffee table, but you're very welcome.'

'Ummm … errrr …' It shouldn't be this awkward, it really

shouldn't. It wasn't like they hadn't socialised before. There had been all those memorable nights out at the pub, the ceilidhs, the walks at the beach, lunches on their days off, tea breaks outside in all weathers, and many, many times where they'd lingered over small talk while he was supposed to be closing up and she was supposed to be heading home. Times she'd missed the bus because she was enjoying his company too much to hurry for it, and she knew he'd always offer to take her home in his faithful old Range Rover. But tonight ... well, it just felt weird.

And he must have read her face, because his eyebrows drew together and he looked at her curiously. 'Are you sure you're okay, Ivy?'

'No. No, I'm not okay. I think I will come in, if the offer's still there.'

'Of course it is!' He looked surprised and stepped back further so she could enter the house.

Despite the size and modern slant to the place, it was homely and Ivy loved everything about it. She knew exactly where everything was and headed straight into the kitchen. She was also horribly aware that the chance to spend time like this with Zac, time where they could chat over a cuppa in the kitchen, was precious – because God alone knew when she'd see him again if she was in Glasto. It wasn't like she'd be a twenty-minute drive away.

'So, what's up?' Zac followed her into the kitchen and flicked the kettle on. He smiled one of his slow smiles and his eyes twinkled briefly. 'It's not often the boss makes a cuppa, so appreciate this one, aye?'

Despite herself, Ivy laughed as she shrugged her coat off. Hanging it on the back of a chair, she sat down at the table and rested her chin in her hands, watching Zac make the drinks. 'That's a lie and you know it.'

'Aye. Maybe.' He grinned and brought the mugs over. Sitting down opposite her, he pushed hers across the table, and she accepted it gratefully. 'Probably best in here with it. Like I say, the coffee table's a mess. I was reading the paperwork for Taigh Fallon and had an in-depth conversation with Angel. She's volunteered to come up and see it with me. Said she'd be up Monday ... Monday? Aye. Monday, I think.' He nodded vaguely and Ivy hid a smile behind her mug. *Typical Zac.* Then the smile slid off her face as she remembered why she was here.

She sighed; nothing for it but to come out with it. 'It's nice she's doing that for you. Hopefully I'll get to meet her at last. Anyway – I wanted to come and tell you this face to face.' She took a deep breath. 'I've got the chance to go to Glastonbury in the summer.' She watched his face carefully for any reaction. Anything at all.

Zac was quiet for a few seconds, clearly deep in thought. Then he nodded. 'Aye. You deserve a holiday. You've worked hard enough. When is it? I'll get someone in to cover.' He smiled at her encouragingly. 'It's a long way down, that, mind. You renting a car? Or going by train?'

'Zac! No. No, it's not a holiday. It's ... it's ... oh Zac.' She heard her voice break. 'I've got the chance of a studio down there. It's a dream come true. Honestly, I just got a call about it tonight. If it works out, I'll be living down there.'

'Hang on. You're going down there to *live*? Ivy!' There was an expression in his eyes, the briefest flicker of something; then the shutters came down. Zac nodded, his face perfectly composed – apart from maybe, just maybe, a twitch of a muscle in his jaw. Then even that was gone. 'Well, if it's a dream come true, you have to go. When? When will you be leaving?'

Ivy stared at him, unable to respond. She hadn't expected a declaration of undying love, but she had expected – *something*. Something more than a brief flicker of emotion and a calm acceptance.

Or maybe she had just hoped for that.

Eventually she found her voice. 'I don't know when I'll be going. It's not written in stone, but I've got a few weeks left. Maybe a month or two.' She shrugged, not knowing the answer really. 'But I wanted to speak to you first before I committed myself.'

'But it's the chance of a new life, eh? And I know it's a chance you've set your heart upon.' There was a remoteness in his tone that she hadn't heard before. It made her uncomfortable.

'Aye, but if you have any reason—' She stopped. She didn't think she could continue without bursting into tears. She hadn't really rehearsed this. She certainly hadn't expected Zac to close down quite as quickly as he had either. She focused on her half-drunk coffee to avoid looking at him.

Oh God. This was awful. What a mess.

Ivy lifted her eyes from the depths of the mug to find him watching her. Again, there was that funny little expression in his eyes. He smiled; a small, sad sort of smile. Then he took a deep breath and nodded. 'Ivy. I could never come between you and your dreams. Go. Please. Just go, and come back if you have to. Your job will be here if you want it. I ...' His voice trailed off, and he shifted his focus to somewhere over her shoulder. 'I'll miss you. But you should go. When the chance eventually comes, you should take it. You've got plenty of time yet, though. Not until summer. That's a while away yet ...'

She waited, almost not daring to breathe for his next sentence.

But the next sentence, the sentence she wanted to hear, never came.

And she knew, right then, she was going to Glastonbury and nobody was going to make an attempt to stop her.

She thought she might have felt a little happier at that prospect.

After Zac had driven Ivy home, in an entirely awkward silence that made him, at least, miserable, he pulled back up at the croft and looked at the two empty coffee mugs. He hadn't seen that coming, not at all. In his mind, Ivy was a permanent fixture at his place – as permanent as the sea on the horizon and the mountains in the distance. He had never, ever contemplated the fact she might leave. She fitted in there like the missing piece of a puzzle.

He knew, of course, that it was her dream to go to Glastonbury and experience life down there. He had done much the same when he had come to Skye to follow his dream. But he'd kind of hoped that once she'd settled on the Isle of Skye, she would love it as much as he did and not want to go away after all.

How naïve he'd been. What on earth did he expect? It was her decision at the end of the day, not his.

But still ...

What the hell was he going to do without her?

However, he was right; he knew he was right, painful as it

41

might be. He had to let her go, and pray to the ancient gods of that sea and those mountains that she'd come back. Surely Ivy living in Glastonbury was not and was never going to be a permanent arrangement? She'd only been here a relatively short time, but, to Zac, it already felt like she belonged here.

He could only hope so anyway.

When a pretty, dark-haired girl pulled up at the workshop on Monday with an extraordinarily pale face and extraordinarily black eye make-up, Ivy knew exactly who it would be. She smiled a welcome, although her smile still felt a little wobbly, even though her decision was made and she'd spoken at length to Gideon over the weekend. He said he was going to come back to her with a date, and it all sounded like it was heading in the right direction. Which, as she acknowledged again, a few months ago would have been amazing.

There was absolutely no point dwelling on it though; Zac was happy for her to go, and that was great. Truly it was.

However.

'You have to be Angel,' Ivy said, pulling herself together and smiling at the newcomer. 'I feel like I already know you. Zac's always talking about you.'

'And *you* must be Ivy.' The oddly-vintage, yet thoroughly modern, dark-haired woman smiled back at her and spoke in a gorgeous Yorkshire accent, which seemed at odds with her Victorian Gothic Heroine look. *Although*, Ivy mused, *Catherine Earnshaw probably spoke with a Yorkshire accent in* Wuthering Heights – *seeing as it was set on the Yorkshire moors.* She blinked and shook her head as if to clear the weird thoughts that this girl had inspired in her, and was secretly delighted when Angel continued by saying, 'I've heard a lot about you too. It's great to meet you at last.' Then, to Ivy's surprise, Angel gave her a huge hug, before stepping backwards and looking at her searchingly. 'Are you going then? *Really* going to Glasto? Zac mentioned you might be considering it.'

'Sorry? What ... well. Aye. Aye, I am. At some point. My friend Gideon says there's a pretty good chance of getting somewhere in summer.' Verbalising it made her stomach churn, and the delighted feeling of a moment ago floated across the fields and up the Cuillins, never to be seen again, it seemed. In truth, part of Ivy was desperate to go and join Gideon, but another part of her really, really didn't want to leave Zac.

Her eyes drifted over to the workshop, and Angel followed her gaze. 'Ah-ha. Yep. It's like that then. Exactly like that. You know, I love Zac but he's incredibly stupid at times. Has he tried to change your mind? Asked you to stay?'

'Ummm – no. No. Not in so many words ...'

Ivy pulled a face, thinking about it all, and Angel rolled her eyes heavenwards, apparently understanding. 'Good grief. That is totally unsurprising. He doesn't want you to go, you know. I'm pretty sure of it. He told me you bake cakes and everything. Oh, and that your jewellery is amazing.'

'Oh – thanks. I love your jewellery too, that necklace is gorgeous. Zac says you're really talented. Jet must be fun to work with?'

'It is indeed. And thank you.' Angel grinned, then tilted her head on one side and studied Ivy. 'Yes. He's an idiot. Leave him with me for a few days. I'll try to talk to him when I have him captive on the mainland. But first, let me pop in and surprise him. He'll be sucked into whatever he's doing, and I love making him jump.' She laughed and clapped her hands, and Ivy knew she was teasing.

She let Angel go and watched her sashay into the workshop, imagining the scene inside.

She would miss the place, she really would.

But the idea of a little studio of her own, something just like this, was a chance not to be missed.

And she didn't have to stay, did she, if it didn't work out?

But she knew, deep down, that she had to give it a go.

Chapter Five

Zac and Angel had made it to Taigh Fallon, on the dreaded mainland, and after the appropriate excitement from Angel and the expected dour glares from Zac, they were exploring the grounds of the old house, walking on the shores of the Loch.

Zac was telling Angel about Jeanie, and, even as he talked, he realised how wonderful the old lady had been. He was starting to feel a little guilty about the thoughts he was having about being lumbered with Taigh Fallon, and had sworn several times that he'd be returning to Skye that evening. Angel had other ideas; to his horror, he'd found out that she'd packed an overnight bag for him as well. He had no intention of opening the damn thing though; he wouldn't be staying on the mainland any longer than he had to.

To be fair, he truly didn't feel he belonged on the mainland, and especially not at Taigh Fallon. But part of it, a part that he was trying to hide – quite unsuccessfully, it had to be said – even from himself, was because he wanted to spend every precious moment with Ivy that he could before she went away – perhaps forever. Still, they had until summer.

'She was a character.' Zac shrugged, talking about his beloved Great Aunt Jeanie again, as he bent down on the stony shore of the Loch. He picked up a pebble and weighed it in his hand before skimming it across the surface of the water. 'But there are more of us than just me, and I'm pretty

45

sure my cousin Kyle will appear once he's been informed. Which is why I can't get excited about Taigh Fallon. It's not properly mine. It has to be shared, but God knows how we'll do that. What if someone appears out of the woodwork years after this place gets sold?'

'It sounds as if Jeanie made it pretty clear what she wanted,' said Angel. 'The solicitors will have it all in hand.'

'I suppose.' Zac folded his arms and stared out at the Loch. 'You get a good view of Eilean Donan here, don't you?'

'Beautiful. I spotted it before. All the bedrooms on the west look out onto it.'

Zac cast her a glance. 'You've already been in the bedrooms?'

'When I was doing my walkabout. They've all got little en suites too, which is so lovely. I've already chosen my room.' She looked smug and far too innocent.

'Why does that not surprise me?' He grinned, feeling a rush of affection for his best friend. They knew each other inside out, good and bad, and he knew their bond was unbreakable. Good-naturedly, he pushed her. 'Oh Angel, why did it never work out between us? I know everything about you and it should have been easy.'

Angel laughed. 'I know. Maybe that's why it didn't; we know each other too well. It's the "friend zone" thing. And you're far too nice for me. I wouldn't be able to argue with you.'

'You're probably right. There's no magic, no spark. Just Angel and Zac. A and Z with no in-betweens.'

Angel nodded in agreement. It was the plain truth, after all. She picked up a handful of stones, clearly preparing to skim them over the water; she was better at it than him and used to, annoyingly, count every skim, until one day he'd threatened to chuck her pile of stones in the sea if she didn't shut up about it. 'Do you think you'll ever get that spark?' Angel asked him. 'With anyone?' Her voice was suspiciously innocent and he shot a glance at her. Angel was *never* innocent.

'I hope so,' he said, guardedly. He didn't know where this was going, but he had a good idea and his heart began thumping. He watched as Angel took aim and sent a smooth grey pebble bouncing across the water five times. 'Nice one.' He'd allow her that. Anything to divert her.

'Thanks.' The next one only made it four times. 'Do you think you could see yourself with someone like Ivy?' The diversion hadn't worked. Angel looked askance at him and watched as he considered it. He knew the answer, but damn her, he wasn't going to give into her that easily.

'I don't know.' He pushed his hair away from his forehead, his too-long fringe flattened by the steady drizzle. 'I don't suppose she'd be interested.' He frowned. He wouldn't give her any more than that. No way. She was too perceptive and it was a rabbit hole he didn't want to explore today.

'Why ever not? Six times! Hurrah!'

Damn her!

'Show off. Here, let me. Three. Not bad.' But it still wasn't enough to distract her. He could practically feel her dark, curious eyes drilling into him, waiting for an answer. 'I don't know – I suspect because she's got ambitions of her own and itchy feet and doesn't want to settle on a Scottish island.' He was being cagey, and he knew it.

'You know this how?' Angel turned to him, wiping her hands down her skirt, leaving streaks of mud and silt on the black fabric.

'It's obvious, isn't it?' He sighed. Time to admit it. 'She's clever and she's pretty and she's talented. I told you she's wanting to go to Glastonbury. She does painting, and I've also already told you that she bakes the most phenomenal cakes.' He grinned. 'Jeanie would have enjoyed them, I think. Ivy's interested in her crystals and her holistic therapies, and what use could they be where I live?'

'You said the same when you didn't know how successful the tea room would be. That's taken you by surprise – so maybe she could use her skills to help you build your business? Like you hoped.'

'She's just renting in the town, though.'

'Renting is easy enough for her to give up.'

'Maybe, but don't forget she's originally from the mainland.'

'So bloody what?' cried Angel. 'I despair of you. I really do.'

Zac just shook his head, then lifted his wrist and checked his watch. It was *really* time to knock this conversation on the head. 'I think you're wrong, Angel, whatever ideas you may be concocting in that little gothy head of yours. But regardless, I need to get back to Skye. It's getting late and it'll take a while.' He looked up and was aware that Angel followed his gaze. The sky seemed lower than it had been; great, thick banks of cloud building up and the rain was definitely getting heavier. 'You know, I don't even know if I'm happy leaving you. It's a big old strange house.'

Angel shook her head. It seemed there was nothing better to her than being marooned in a big old strange house, entirely on her own, in a setting that wouldn't look out of place in a creepy old novel. 'And the landline is working, and there's a decent enough mobile signal, so it's not like I'll be cut off.' She pressed her lips together in that stubborn gesture Zac had often despaired of when she was certain she knew best.

'Even so. I'm not sure. You should probably come back with me. I'd be glad of the company anyway.' *Because if you're prattling away next to me, it'll stop me thinking so much about Ivy and what the hell I'll do when I don't see her practically every bloody day ...*

'Oh, dearest Zac.' Angel flung her arms around him, almost unbalancing them both. He teetered on the edge of the Loch, remembering all too well being pushed in it when he was a child by the elusive Canadian cousin. Zac was twenty-nine now, and the memory was still clear. It had been a bloody cold loch!

'I'm *staying*.' Angel was insisting. 'You can collect me tomorrow. But I think you should stay too.'

'I think I should go. *We* should go. Last chance – you coming back?'

'Nope.' She shook her head and released him.

Zac knew when he was beaten. He gave up trying to persuade her, smiled and dropped a quick, friendly kiss on her forehead, then took her arm. 'Come on then. I'll haul you up that mud bank and make sure you're okay before I leave properly. It's no use arguing with you, is it?'

'No use at all.' Angel allowed herself to be guided up the mud bank. A low rumble of thunder sounded far away and he felt her jump. The rain began to come down harder.

'Now is probably a good time to start running,' Zac observed.

'You're right.' She shook his arm off, picked up her long

skirt and, lowering her head, ran as fast as she could towards Taigh Fallon. Zac followed at a jog, taking one last look at the glowering clouds behind him.

He couldn't help but wonder whether that particular storm had come in from Skye, and whether those same rain clouds had blotted out the light above his croft, and rained on Ivy.

The thought made him shiver, but he wasn't quite sure why ...

But, as it transpired, it appeared as if someone had a higher plan for him anyway – because that very evening, his faithful 4×4 decided not to work.

It seemed as if he was marooned on the mainland as well as Angel.

Grumbling loudly, Zac popped the bonnet and climbed out of the immobile vehicle. 'My engine might be flooded. Literally,' he said to Angel, who wasn't doing a very good job of hiding her elation. He poked around as the rain fell in big, fat drops down the back of his neck and he swore. 'I could ring the recovery service. I suppose.' Zac looked up at the darkening sky. 'But if I don't do it soon, I doubt they'll even come out in this.'

'They come anywhere at any time, but why bother? You're right. Just leave it tonight and call them tomorrow.' Angel was wheedling. 'Do you really want to be driving all that way home in this stuff anyway?' She let the raindrops drench her outstretched hand. 'Live a little, Zachary. Please.'

Zac slammed the bonnet down and scowled at the sky. 'It certainly does seem as if this is in for the night.'

'Then that's a good enough reason for you to hole up here with me. Look at it. You're not even going to get two hundred yards out of that thing tonight, never mind all the way home to Skye. Good car.' She patted the scratched navy-blue bonnet.

'Good car?' Zac snorted in disgust. 'Pile of junk, more like it. I guess I'm with you for the evening then.' He frowned. 'And I guess I need to call Ivy to let her know.' He tried to keep his voice neutral. 'She'll need to close up, and goodness knows where that leaves me for tomorrow.' His heart thudded a little quicker at the thought he'd be talking to her soon – talking to her with a valid reason, not just because he missed her and wanted to hear her voice. God forbid she ever thought that – he wouldn't want to be the reason she ditched her chance in Glastonbury because, much as he didn't want her to go, neither did he want to crush her dreams.

'Surely she can open up as well?' The issue was clearly *not* an issue with Angel. 'I'm positive she's competent enough to do that.'

'She might feel it's an imposition, or that I've done it deliberately.' *Why on earth was he putting obstacles in the way of an innocent call? What on earth would even make her think that?* Honestly, he needed to get a grip. This was one of the reasons he didn't like the mainland. Rational thinking seemed to go out of the window.

'She'll think nothing of the sort.' Angel had spoken, the voice of reason. 'Just call her, explain about the car and she'll be fine.' A shrug. Nothing was a bother.

'Hmmm,' muttered Zac. 'I'm still going to apologise to her.' The rain was relentlessly falling, dripping off the leaves and creating puddles beneath the trees. 'I'll just tell her it's real Scottish rain and she'll understand,' he said ironically.

He didn't really mind spending the evening with Angel

– but part of him had definitely been looking forward to returning to his croft.

And to Ivy.

'So,' Angel said, throwing the comment over her shoulder as she practically danced back to the house, completely oblivious to his churning emotions, 'which bedroom do you want? You can have any of them, so long as I get the first one on the left of the staircase.'

'So, there it is.' Zac's voice on the phone from the mainland sounded tired and cross, and Ivy didn't blame him. 'My car won't work and I'm stuck here. I'm sorry.'

She looked at the phone curiously. 'What on earth are you sorry about?'

'I'm sorry about the fact that I'm *genuinely* stuck here and I'm going to have to impose on you. Would you keep an eye on things for me back home, please? The tea room, the studio and all that?'

Home. That word. Skye was home for now, but in a few months home would be Glastonbury. She gave herself a mental shake. Glastonbury was good! It was a dream come true! Zac's home was here, on Skye, and always would be. This was where he had his croft and his business. She would be doing exactly the same, only in the south west of England as opposed to the north west of Scotland.

Ivy did wonder what Zac would do about Taigh Fallon but reasoned that with the irrepressible Angel by his side, the trip would be rather memorable to say the least.

'It's all in good hands with me, Zac,' she said. 'Don't worry about a thing. I'll come early tomorrow to open up. I'll get a taxi in.'

'No!' She opened her eyes wide, startled at the force of his denial. 'No. Look – there's a spare key for my croft on the tea room bunch. Just camp out in my place tonight, save yourself the journey. Honestly. The second bedroom is made up with clean sheets on the bed, but don't go in the small one as Ange'll have left it like a midden.'

'Zac! Are you sure?'

'Completely. If you're okay doing that? I mean—' he sounded contrite '—if you've got nothing else on. It's bad of me to assume. Sorry. Forget I said it. A taxi will be fine, I'll give you the cash when—'

'No!' This time, it was the force of her sentiment that surprised her. 'No. Really. I'd be happy to stay. If you trust the place to me?'

'Of course I do.' He sounded relieved. 'Good. Like I say, I'm sorry. I would have let you know sooner, if the car hadn't broken down right now.'

'Don't be daft.' She looked across the car park to the croft and smiled. It was almost perfect. She had a shepherd's pie ready to heat up for tea at home, but that was nothing to fret about.

The only thing that would have made staying at the croft overnight absolutely perfect, was if Zac had been there with her.

She felt her cheeks heat up at the thought and clapped one cool palm to her burning face. *Goodness me.* If the thought of spending the night at his place had her feeling like this when he wasn't even there, then she hated to think what her reaction would be if they were ever in that situation together – like perhaps if they got snowed in, in one of the wild blizzards that would come across from nowhere … her face ignited even more.

Then, as if Zac had read her mind, he suddenly asked, 'Ivy, what's the weather been like there this afternoon?'

'The weather?' She frowned and looked over at the mountains. 'Well, we had some black clouds roll in, and they dumped a pile of rain on us before heading inland ... hey!' She grinned. 'Maybe the rain you've had there is the same storm. Snap!'

'Snap indeed. Aye.' His voice was warm. 'Look. I have to go now, but hopefully I'll see you tomorrow, okay? Help yourself to anything you need. The food and the contents of the liquor cabinet are yours for the taking.'

'Okay. Thanks. I'll try not to over-indulge. Bye for now then.'

'Bye. I trust you. And thanks again.'

She was still smiling as she went back to work.

The rest of the day passed quite pleasantly. The tea room trade was steady but not overwhelming, and she pinned a note on the door of the workshop asking potential customers to seek her out if they needed any help. And so it was quite cheerfully that she locked up the business side of Zac's premises, located the key to the croft and let herself in.

She'd made herself something to eat, had a hot bath and was wrapped in Zac's towelling robe with a cup of tea at her elbow, contemplating what to watch on TV while the washing machine did a quick load of her clothing, when her mobile rang again.

She smiled, stretching out for it, expecting it to be Zac checking in with her – but this time, the call was from Gideon. And she knew she absolutely had to take it.

'Gid! I don't hear from you for ages, and here we are, chatting twice within a week.'

'Yeah. Cool, isn't it?' Gid laughed. 'Good reason to call, though. The studio's available in like two weeks.'

'Two weeks!' Ivy sat up and stared at the TV screen, not really aware of what the moving figures were doing. 'But that's hardly any time at all!'

'I know! So you don't even have to wait until summer. Just hand in your notice like ASAP, and come down. It'll be amazing, I promise. I can't wait for you to be here. It'll be just like old times.'

'Aye. Old times.' Ivy recalled the many years she'd known Gid. He was one of her best friends, and the fact they had done a student placement together at Glastonbury had solidified their bond. She trusted him, and if he was excited about the prospect of her relocating, then that had to be a positive thing. A little squiggle of nervous excitement rippled through her, and for the first time she wondered if the Fates were conspiring to get her down there to experience it all. It had been such a dream of hers, for so very long. And sometimes it was good to step out of your comfort zone, wasn't it?

If she didn't do it now, she'd regret it. She had to, at the very least, give it a go and get it out of her system. Zac hadn't made it particularly clear whether he would ever consider her more than a friend and colleague – so, being brutal about it, it might do them both good if she went away for a little while. Put some space between them, let things be for now.

Ivy was, as always, a great believer in Fate, and much as she wanted to stay here on Skye, with Zac, she also wanted to experience her dream in Glastonbury.

And she would have to trust that if it was meant to be with her and Zac, it would be so.

She took a deep breath and closed her eyes. 'Okay, Gid. I'll take it. Let's start planning.'

At Taigh Fallon the next day, Zac felt out of sorts and positively grumpy.

A commotion in the night had resulted in an unexpected intruder – who had ended up actually being an expected intruder: his cousin, Kyle, fresh from Canada. To be fair, he maybe wasn't expected to turn up in the middle of a stormy night, but he had done, and to be honest, it was a night Zac really didn't want to spend too long picking over.

Suffice it to say, Angel was in a furious temper, Kyle was in an even more furious temper, and Zac had to put up with soothing both a shockingly bad-tempered Yorkshire lass, who was positively quivering and fizzing with righteous indignation, and an irritable Canadian, who was storming around the place, under Angel's influence, with a face like thunder. The crunch had come when Kyle, with a curl of his Byronic lips, had called Angel "Morticia", and she'd decided to spend the night exuding hatred towards Kyle, in Zac's bed. They'd shared a bed on many occasions – completely platonically – and that particular night was no exception. The truth of the matter was that Zac had been too tired to even complain and send her packing; even if she'd been happy to go back to her own room.

As a result, an exhausted Zac was staring at his 4×4 quite miserably when he heard Angel approaching.

He turned to greet her and frowned, at odds with the whole situation really. 'It's not looking good,' he said morosely, gesturing to his poor car. 'It needs some parts. It could take a good few hours to get them. They have to go and source them or something.' He waved his hand dismissively. 'Whatever it is, I can't go anywhere fast. I strongly suspect I'm going to be stuck here for another night.'

Angel patted Zac on the arm. 'At least it's not terminal. You'll soon be back on Skye. Have you told Ivy yet?'

Zac shook his head. 'I need to call her. She'll be waiting for me.'

'Then call her. And while you've got the phone, call your bloody solicitor and get your bloody cousin disinherited.'

'What?' Zac stared at her. 'You can't be serious, Angel. I'm not going to do that!'

Angel sighed. 'I *know*, Zac. But I wish you *could* do that. He's very obnoxious ...'

Her tirade about Kyle continued, until eventually, for the sake of peace, Zac withdrew his phone from his pocket and held it up. 'I'll call Ivy,' he said. 'Anything to get you off my back.'

And so, after deflecting even more animosity between his friend and his cousin, who chose that exact moment to come growling around the corner and challenge Angel about snooping around in a secret corridor or some such nonsense, Zac called her. 'Ivy? I'm still stuck on the mainland.' Zac pulled a face. 'They need parts for the car. They said it could be a few hours. They're going to tow it to the garage.'

'A few hours? Will you get back tonight then?'

'No, I doubt it. But I've got a problem regardless. I don't feel right leaving Angel here, but I don't think she wants to come back to Skye just yet. She'd love a few more days ... but there's stuff going on.'

'Oh! Is there anything I can do?' Ivy sounded concerned and Zac smiled, thinking of her furrowing her brow.

'Not unless you come here and save Angel's soul from eternal damnation.'

'What?' This time she sounded shocked.

'Well, it's just that my cousin's turned up from Canada. You might remember I said he was left part of the house as well – it's pretty complicated, but it appears that Angel and Kyle don't get on very well. Actually, they don't get on at all. I think she's going to murder him before long. I can tell.'

'Really? What do you mean by "don't get on"?'

'They argue. *Constantly*. She really hates him.'

'Hate is a strong word, Zac.' She sounded amused.

'Believe me. It's truly hate.'

'Hmm. You know what they say though, don't you?'

'No. What?'

'Hate is very close to love.'

Zac laughed. '*Wheesht*! There's no way that's on the cards! It's like a battle of words and wills the whole time. They've only had about twelve hours in each other's company as well.'

'Aye.' There was another pause. 'I suppose that's not the way for everyone, but it suits some people. I think it's called passion. *Wuthering Heights* and all that.'

'Seriously? I couldn't be bothered with all that. They're a pair, all right – both as dark as the Earl of Hell's waistcoat! But it wouldn't be for me.'

'What *could* you be bothered with then, Zac?' Her voice was amused.

Zac stared at the phone. It was a very good question. He opened his mouth to reply, then closed it again.

The moment was lost though, as Ivy spoke. 'Oh – some post came today.' There was a rustle and a clatter as she put the phone down to, presumably, sort the post out. 'It's from the solicitor, I think. It's a truly official looking envelope.'

'I'll get it when I come back. It's probably to tell me they've located Kyle.'

'I think, from what you say, you located him first!'

'He located Taigh Fallon before that. And now—' Zac looked over his shoulder '—I can hear them arguing about this secret corridor. Again.'

'Secret corridor?'

'Apparently we have one. Kyle found it, Angel went in afterwards, and I think they are both trying to lay claim to it. Or they might be complaining about the fact that each one of them has been in it without the other one's permission. Or perhaps they just want to brick each other up in it.'

'It sounds very much like they don't know what they want with anything.'

'You're probably right. Anyway, I'm sorry I won't be back sooner. Can you manage for another day if you need to?'

'I'm sure I can, but there's something I need to talk to you about when you do get back.'

'Okay. Do I need to worry?'

'Ha! No, not too much.'

Zac's toes curled. Her nonchalance seemed to be rather forced. And he knew – he just *knew*...

'It's just ... I've got the chance to go back to Glastonbury sooner than I thought, and I'm considering doing it. It just means that you'll need a new assistant quite quickly ... if I do go.'

His toes ceased curling, and it was his stomach's turn to

drop to the ground. 'Oh. Right. I kind of thought it wasn't so ... imminent.'

'It wasn't meant to be, but the chance has come up for a studio. I have to take it.'

'I suspect you do.' He let the words sink in. So, it was now "sooner" rather than "later" when she'd be going. That wasn't good. Not good at all. But what could he do? *Nothing*. His voice sounded almost as fakely cheerful as hers as he continued. 'But you won't be gone by tomorrow, will you? So I'll still see you then, aye?'

'Aye.'

Zac looked up at the blue sky breaking out over Eilean Donan and frowned at nothing in particular, thinking about his car, thinking about Ivy and Glastonbury. 'That's if I get back.' Oh, he hoped he'd get back, he hoped it so much. 'Right. I'll call you tomorrow, okay? From wherever I am, and let you know what's happening. If it's too late, Angel will just force me to stay another night anyway.'

'The place isn't going to run away,' replied Ivy. There was a genuine smile in her voice now.

'No,' said Zac. 'It's not.'

But you might.

A couple of days later, Ivy was ten minutes away from shutting the doors of the tea room, taking the opportunity to run a cloth around the tables and collect up the last few pieces of discarded crockery.

There was suddenly an almighty *slam* and the door flew back on its hinges, setting the welcoming little bell ringing like a campanologist on speed was in charge of it.

'Angel!' At first, Ivy wasn't sure it was the perfectly turned out girl she'd seen on Monday, but as she looked more closely, she could see that it was indeed Angel Tempest, drenched through from the Skye rain, her hair sticking to her head, her make-up running and wearing a scowl that would terrify the devil himself.

'Ivy. I don't suppose Zac is back, is he?' asked Angel.

An internal butterfly flapped its wings madly somewhere in the region of Ivy's stomach at the thought, but she made a great effort to give nothing away to Angel. 'Ummm … no. Should he be?'

Angel shook her head helplessly, then exploded. 'Oh, sod it. I'll be honest. I hate Kyle Fallon and I've run away from Taigh Fallon. I know Zac isn't back. My phone is switched off because I didn't want the hassle, so I'll switch it back on and see how many missed calls I have.'

'Okay.' This Kyle situation was obviously exactly as Zac had described it. 'There's enough coffee left in the percolator if you want one. You look like you could use some caffeine,' she offered.

'Thank you. That would be lovely.' Angel threw herself into the closest seat and, switching her phone on, began to scroll. Ivy saw her stab out a number and hold the phone up to her ear. Studying Angel more closely as she prepared a mug of strong black coffee and gave it to her, she saw the girl was even paler beneath her make-up and looked as if she had been crying.

There was an indignant quacking from Angel's phone as Zac answered, seemingly immediately, and Angel's scowl deepened as she spoke. 'In your tea room,' she told the phone. 'Drinking your coffee which Ivy very kindly offered me.'

Ah. He wanted to know where she was then. Ivy hovered

by the counter, judging her moment. The conversation raged on for a few minutes, then Angel's shoulders dropped and she looked calmer.

'Thanks,' Angel said. 'Do you want to speak to Ivy?' Then she looked up at Ivy and smiled wanly as Ivy eventually chanced sitting down opposite her with a cup of tea.

Ivy strained to hear the response, but assumed it must have been "no" as Angel disconnected the call, looked at the mobile and tossed it onto the table with a sigh. Then she looked up at Ivy in sudden horror. 'You know – I *really* hope Zac wasn't giving bloody Kyle a lift …'

'Why would that matter?' Ivy was curious now.

'Because he was on bloody speakerphone, that's why. God. Imagine that. More ammunition for the horrible creature.'

'Who's horrible? Zac?'

'What? No! No, not Zac at all. Zac is the sweetest, if not the most frustrating man on the planet. Actually, no. He's not the most frustrating man on the planet. Kyle is. His horrible Canadian cousin.'

'Ah.' Ivy thought it wise to say nothing more.

'Has Zac told you about Kyle?'

'Only that his cousin turned up and you two were arguing.' She risked a grin, and Angel suddenly laughed.

'Oh yeah. We've been arguing all right. Kyle is dreadful. I love Zac deeply dearly, but, my word, I could shake him at times. You?'

'What?' Ivy was caught unawares at the direct comment and slopped a little of her tea out of the mug. 'Sorry – what do you mean?'

'I mean,' said Angel resting her chin in her hands and seemingly appraising Ivy, 'that he can't see what's under his nose. Like that lovely house. And what his horrible cousin is trying to do. And you as well, I bet. He can't see *you*. But he says you're definitely going to Glastonbury?'

'Aye, that's right. I was hoping to go in the summer, but Gideon – my friend down there – he called and told me it would be more like a fortnight.'

'A fortnight from now?'

'Aye, from now.'

'And does Zac know?'

Ivy nodded slowly. 'Aye. I told him.'

'And?'

'And,' she shrugged, not meeting Angel's eyes, 'he said he'd still see me when he came back. But he's not back yet, and I'm not sure *when* he will be back.' Her gaze slid to the bunch of keys on the table. 'I was staying over in the croft, so it was a bit easier to cover for him. It's a nice place. But I'll be going home tonight. I was going to wait until he turned up, but if you're here … well, it sounds like you need to speak to him more urgently than I do.'

'Thanks, Ivy. I'm sure he'd *much* rather have you welcome him home to Skye. He really will not want to hear what I say to him.' She pressed her lips together thinly and scowled for a second or two. 'Anyway. He said you had a spare set of keys. Is it okay if I borrow them after you lock up and go and make myself presentable?'

'Oh! Of course. You don't need to ask. Here – do you know which ones they are?'

Angel nodded and pointed to the relevant key. 'It's that one for the front door. I'll wash up these mugs if you want to go and lock everywhere else up, and I'll meet you back outside the tea room.'

'That sounds like a plan. Thanks, Angel.'

'Oh, no worries.' Angel sighed theatrically. 'He really is *stupid*.'

And it seemed as if that was Angel's last word on the subject, but Ivy wasn't actually sure whether "he" referred to Kyle or, more likely, poor old Zac.

By the time Zac returned to his croft later that evening, the place was deserted. His heart sunk as he realised Ivy must have gone home. As he let himself in to the house, it seemed that Angel had made *her*self at home. She was curled up in the sun-room at the back of the croft, flicking through a fashion magazine. Her hair was damp, probably the result of long, relaxing bath, and plaited loosely, and she was wearing a black satin wrap over her nightgown.

'Good evening. It seems as if gemstone jewellery is as popular as ever,' she said. 'I'm not surprised Ivy is heading back down south. There'll be a huge market for it in Glastonbury and she's assured of a workspace, thanks to Gideon.'

'Gideon?' The word was out before he could stop himself. 'Who's Gideon?'

'One of her friends.' Angel looked up at Zac and, despite the times he had seen her bare-faced, he was once again briefly startled to see her without her customary make-up. Her clear skin was creamy and her eyes, although very dark and fringed with black lashes (which he knew she had tinted regularly) were bigger somehow without the sharp lines of kohl around them. She looked about fourteen. 'The friend who got her the workspace. *Gideon*.'

'Oh. That's nice,' Zac said. 'Gideon. Well, she could use my workshop. She only has to say.' He flapped his hand around in the general direction of the workshop. 'It's big enough for both of us.' Time to deflect ... he was doing a lot of that recently; right now, he was basically saying the first things that came into his head. The Ivy issue was important, obviously, but this upset with Angel and Kyle needed dealing with immediately. 'Are you going to tell me what happened with Kyle?'

'Nope,' replied Angel. She turned her head back to the magazine and flicked over a page. 'I take it he's not with you anyway. That's good. And there's a letter for you. Ivy said you knew about it.' Angel did a good imitation of Zac's flapping hand, only she flapped hers in the direction of the coffee table.

'Ah yes. Ivy did tell me, and the solicitor mentioned something was on its way to me. This'll be it.' He leaned over to get it and looked sharply at Angel who was still studying the magazine, her face impassive. 'Don't think I'm letting you off without an explanation, no matter how exciting this letter might be,' he warned her. 'Although I doubt it's another property I've inherited as I might have known about that before now.'

Angel shrugged and flicked another page over without looking at him. 'I doubt it will be exciting,' she commented. 'Probably dull as dishwater, especially if it concerns anything about your horrible cousin.'

Zac shook his head. He knew this problem his best friend had with his cousin wasn't going to go away any time soon. And therefore, it was absolutely time to deal with it ...

The next morning, Zac was satisfied he'd done as much as he could about the Angel and Kyle situation. He felt bad at the fact he'd ended up arguing with Angel, but what he'd told her about the plans he and Kyle had made – the plans which she had clearly misinterpreted – had to be said.

Bloody mainland, causing all sorts of issues – *as usual*, he thought irrationally.

And when he prepared to wave Angel off the next day, she still looked a little like a rabbit caught in headlights. Her face was a little paler under the make-up than it had been, her eyes a little more shadowed.

'Am I forgiven?' he asked as he helped her with her luggage, tucking it in the boot of her car.

'Forgiven for what?'

'For suggesting that deep down you might not want to murder my cousin?'

She smiled and he smiled back, relieved. He hated to think of them parting on a bad note.

'You're forgiven. So long as I am. Murder might not be top of my list for him, but he's ridiculously annoying, you've got to grant me that. It's just as well you don't share that part of your genetics, isn't it? Otherwise I couldn't love you best of all. Well, actually, you *can* be quite annoying. But I'm going to leave that point for another day. And I still do love you best of all. Don't forget it.'

Zac laughed and hugged her. 'It's been so nice to see you. It's my turn to come to Whitby next.'

'Hmm.' Angel raised her eyebrows. 'We both know that's not likely to happen. Zachary Fallon on the mainland? God forbid. But you know, The Room has space for an airbed if you do come, so don't let that put you off.'

'Aye.' He was non-committal. The thought of spending any length of time in Angel's weird little room in the attic of Goth

66

Cottage didn't appeal very much at all. Come on, it was on the mainland, as well as everything else it *didn't* have going for it!

Angel laughed, clearly knowing he was nonplussed. She shook her head and gave him one last hug before she slid into her car. 'Well, I have a long drive, so I'm off.'

'No stopover in Edinburgh?'

'No stopover. I just want to get back. You know?' A shadow flickered across her face and Zac nodded. He understood, somehow, that she had a few things to settle in her mind and, for Angel, a long drive was probably as good a place as any to do it.

'Okay, call me en route. Let me know you're safe.'

'Will do.' She shut the door and blew him a kiss. The car pulled away, and he stood at the end of the track waving to her until the car was a dot.

He turned and headed towards the workshop, thinking about the next piece of jewellery he was going to make. He had some amethyst, which would be quite nice set into a Celtic cross and—

'I like Angel.'

He looked up and saw Ivy standing at the door of the tea room. She must have been there to see her off as well, perhaps waving the tartan tea-towel she was now twisting into a sausage shape between her long, pale fingers.

Zac smiled. 'Yes, she's a good friend. I'm pleased you liked her. Next time she comes up, if you're around, you'll have to take her to the village. I'm sure she'd like that – more exciting than being here for her, I suppose. She's stayed at the hotel, obviously, but she doesn't know all the exciting little bits of it. I suppose she had Taigh Fallon to think about this time, so you didn't get a chance to see more of her. I'm sorry.'

Ivy shrugged. 'Don't be sorry. We've exchanged numbers and things. She said I'd probably enjoy Whitby. Do you know, I've never been?' She gazed out at the little track that led away from the croft. 'I'll call in on my way to Glastonbury if I can. Break my journey.'

'What?' Zac stopped and stared at her. 'Glastonbury? You mean it? Honestly – you are definitely going in two weeks or so?'

'Aye.' She began to twist the tea-towel the other way and then shook it out angrily. 'I *am* going, Zac. I've told you several times and I'm not changing my mind. Do I have to hand an official letter in? And how much notice do I have to give?'

'I don't want to accept your notice or your letter. I don't want you heading to Glasto with Gideon. He's probably a hairy beast adorned in hemp and smelling of patchouli.'

Ivy suddenly laughed. 'No, he's not.' She studied Zac for a moment and smiled, her voice softening. 'Maybe it won't be forever, Zac. Maybe I just have to do this. Just to try it. I might yet come back.'

'Hmm.' Zac stared at her, a curious mix of feelings surging around his mind. 'I'll miss you.'

'And I'll miss you. But we'll survive.' She flicked the end of the tea-towel at him and grinned. 'Come on. Let's have a coffee and talk about what you want in a new assistant.'

She turned and headed into the tea room. Zac simply stared after her. There was just one thought he could come up in response to that: *You. I only want you.*

Chapter Six

As the spring nights gradually lightened over those final couple of weeks, the feeling was bittersweet – to Zac, at least.

It meant that Ivy didn't have much time left on Skye before she went. He didn't want to think about that too much. Over the last few days, she'd helped him to employ Effie, a lady in her mid-sixties who was as cheerful and as pleasant as could be – despite not being Ivy McFarlane – and he knew that she'd be a welcome addition to the tea room.

'I got a lot more applications this time around,' he'd mused as he laid the CVs out on one of the café tables, and Ivy had dipped her head and blushed. Zac may have been vague at times, but could also be perceptive if, as Angel told him once, the wind was blowing in the right direction – and he eventually got the truth out of Ivy; that she'd basically sabotaged his original recruitment process.

'I'm sorry,' she said, smiling up at him and clearly not sorry in the slightest. 'But it was my job from the get-go. We both know it.'

'Aye. We do. It was Fate, as you're so fond of saying.' There'd been one of those odd little moments where their eyes locked, but he'd torn his gaze away and returned to studying the CVs, rather than allowed himself to say something that would perhaps stop her achieving her dreams.

He knew he had to let her go, but that didn't mean he was happy about it.

However, what he *could* do was to make each moment they were together count, and today he wanted to spend some time with her doing something he knew she'd remember as well as he did.

So, he put his tools away, locked up the barn and headed over to the tea room, to make a suggestion he hoped she'd like.

Ivy was trying not to think about the fact that there were only a few days left before she headed down to Glastonbury. Most of her belongings were packed back up into the boxes they'd come out of, a little under a year ago. Luckily, the rental cottage had been furnished, so that at least meant she had no furniture to worry about. She had made a pact with herself to soak up every last moment and experience on Skye. Just in case she didn't come back.

But she refused to allow herself to think that she wouldn't, because there would always, always be a special place in her heart for this island.

Zac interrupted her thoughts by, as was his wont, wandering into the tea room and leaning on the door frame. He looked a little uncertain. 'Ivy. Is there anywhere, anywhere at all, that you haven't been yet and that you want to visit?'

Sometimes he just came out with the most random comments, and she knew this was because part of his mind had already thought about the reasoning behind the comment, and the words just kind of came out of his mouth, as if he expected a person to have been reading his mind moments beforehand. This was one of those times, and she accepted it for what it was – including the fact that the uncertain expression had turned into a weird sort of scowl, and his hair was sticking up endearingly all over. It was longer than she'd ever seen it, and he'd obviously been running his hands through it, which, again, she knew was his habit when he was thinking.

'Many places,' she replied. 'I haven't been to most of Europe and have never been to America. I haven't done Australia either.'

Zac laughed, and his expression relaxed. 'Me neither. But no. I didn't mean that. I meant here. On Skye.'

'Oh! Aye. Of course.' She grinned at him. 'I knew that.'

'Aye, you did,' teased Zac. 'So, is there anywhere I can take you tonight? We can take some coffee in a flask and some of that leftover shortbread as well if you fancy. Ange always says I need to be more spontaneous. Not sure about that myself, mind you.'

'Ha! Well, Zac, you're the one who fancies the shortbread. All the time. But all right. Let's be spontaneous. I've never climbed the Cuillins. It's been something that was on my mind to do, oddly enough.'

'The Cuillins it is then.' Zac pushed himself away from the door frame 'I'll give you a hand finishing up in here, and we'll drive across.'

'I'm not really dressed for mountaineering, though.'

'Well you don't have to be. We don't have to climb the things properly, do we? Just go a little way up.'

Which they did. And once they got there, and walked a little way up one of the gentler slopes, they sat closely together on the heather and watched the sun set.

'Do you need to hurry home?' he asked her, his fringe flopping into his face, casting half of it into shadow. 'Or can I persuade you to have the rest of this coffee and maybe some chocolate? I pinched a couple of bars from the display.'

'Nope,' she replied. 'I don't need to hurry home. I think

I'm pretty much already there.' The sky was a myriad of candy-floss pinks and burnt orange and rose-gold; the sun a giant, flaming ball sinking behind the ancient landscape. She had never felt more at peace.

'Really?' He grinned. 'That's good to hear.'

'Well. Right *now* it's pretty nice. Ask me again when it's dark and raining, and I might say I prefer Paris.'

'Paris!' His comment was dismissive. 'Bloody mainland.'

'But bloody *warmer*. And with amazing coffee.'

'I'll take your word for it. But what about Glastonbury? D'you think that'll be like home as well?'

'I hope so. But right now, *this* is home, this hillside and this coffee and these treats and you ... and I desperately want to stay here a bit longer.'

'That's the right thing to say.' Then he handed her a bar of chocolate and broke the last shortbread into two pieces, and they shared it as the last rays of light sank below the horizon.

Chapter Seven

The day she left came far too quickly for Zac.

'Have you got everything sorted then? Everything packed?' Zac looked at Ivy, silhouetted against the Scottish moors, wondering for the hundredth time if he could simply tell her he wasn't accepting her resignation, definitely not, because he really and truly didn't want her to leave.

Then he squashed those feelings down, and scolded himself for being unsupportive and all the rest. At the end of the day, what claim did he have on her? She worked for him, they were good friends; and good friends helped other good friends follow their dreams and spread their wings. Even if said good friend was determined to move to Glastonbury, which currently felt like the other side of the world.

Glastonbury was, as he kept reminding the pair of them, on the mainland, after all.

'Aye. I think so. If there's anything I've forgotten, someone can send it on.' Ivy looked across the car park to the distant Cuillins, and half-smiled. 'I might be back, you know. It might not be forever.'

'Aye. So you've said before.'

'But I'm still going.'

'You're still going.'

'You know I have to, don't you?'

'I know.' *But that doesn't mean I have to like it*, he thought.

'If there's any reason – any *massively* good reason I shouldn't – perhaps you should tell me? Before it really is too late.' She transferred that smile to him, and he very nearly crumbled there and then. 'It might not stop me going, but it might mean I come back sooner rather than later.'

'Is the fact that I'll miss you around the place enough? That I like your artwork and it looks good in my gift shop and I need you to keep it stocked up? Or that I have a feeling my new staff member just won't be as personable as my last one?' He pulled a face, trying to make a joke.

'Personable? Hmm. You'll manage.'

'Aye.' He shoved his hands in his pockets, desperate to hug her to wish her farewell, but terrified that he wouldn't be able to let her go.

'Zac ...' She looked as if she was almost going to say something else, then clamped her lips together.

They stood there awkwardly for what seemed like forever, then he gave in. His hands came out of his pockets and his arms went around Ivy almost at the same time as her arms came around him.

'I'll miss you. I really will,' she whispered against his chest.

'I'll miss you too. But good luck. And all the rest. And I'll see you ... soon. I hope.' He rested his chin on the top of her head and closed his eyes briefly.

'Soon. Yes.'

They broke away and smiled at each other again. Then she nodded and turned away. 'Bye, Zac.'

'Bye, Ivy.'

And Zac didn't think he'd ever get that image out of his head; the image of Ivy McFarlane walking away from him, walking away from Skye, for what might be the very last time.

Chapter Eight

The Isle of Skye, June

Zac wondered for the umpteenth time why he'd thought this would be a good idea. Angel had been in touch, asking whether he'd like to "pop over for a visit" to sit on the beach and watch the sun rise on the Solstice. At first, he'd thought she meant "popping over" to Taigh Fallon, because, since she and Kyle had well and truly resolved their differences, she had been to the property a couple of times now. Zac had helpfully pointed out that there wasn't really a beach at Taigh Fallon unless you counted the loch side.

'Oh no, Zac. I meant *my* beach. At Whitby.'

'You don't have a beach either,' he'd said. 'I think you'll find it's a public facility.'

'Hmm. Whatever. Are you coming?'

'No thank you.'

'I thought you'd say that. So I'm coming to you. Is that okay?'

'What? Who's coming where?'

'Me. I'm coming to you. Hurrah! And I thought you might like the company.'

'I'm fine, thanks,' he replied dryly. 'And I thought you hated the Summer Solstice.'

'Don't be silly. I absolutely don't hate it. I just get miserable about the days getting shorter. I know it's better for the Gothic atmosphere at Whitby blah blah blah, and I do love a good old storm, as we both know, but I need sunshine as well to thrive, you see. *Sunshine*! Anyway. You miss Ivy, any fool can tell that. And Ivy says Ashaig beach is just amazing.'

Zac clamped his lips together. He wasn't going to admit that he missed Ivy – but he couldn't help asking the next question. 'Is Ivy coming up too?'

'Ivy? Of course not! She's got the Solstice down there in Glastonbury to keep her busy. Anyway, I want to see you. I want to make sure you're all right.'

He half-smiled. 'I told you, I'm fine. And anyway, the Solstice is tomorrow. Isn't it?'

'Yes. That's why I'm leaving Taigh Fallon this afternoon to come over to see you. Surprise!'

It was one hell of a surprise. Which was why Zac was currently making up Angel's pokey little room in his croft and cursing under his breath. Sometimes he enjoyed having such a spontaneous friend. Sometimes, like today, it was not so enjoyable. He stood up and looked out of the window at the sea.

Ashaig beach was certainly a beautiful place. He and Ivy had gone there a couple of times when she was still getting to know Skye. He'd shown her the little stone-built well house that covered the sacred spring at Ashaig, allegedly created when St Maelrubha had sailed over from Applecross and the saint had torn a small tree from the ground.

'I don't get how he sailed over on a big stone, though,' Ivy had mused, looking out at the sea and the island of Pabay, where the good saint was supposed to have settled. 'Surely he'd sink.'

'Heathen,' Zac had said mildly, and Ivy had laughed. She'd squatted down and taken a handful of sand from the beach, letting it run through her fingers. Silhouetted against

Beinn na Caillich, one of the red Cuillin Mountains, with the wind blowing her hair loose, Zac had thought her absolutely a spirit of the Island and, just for a moment, he'd been completely mesmerised by her.

Then the moment was lost as she'd stood up and grinned at him, and said, 'This place reminds me a lot of Glastonbury. There's such a wonderful, sacred feeling to the springs there too ... It makes me realise how spiritual nature is.'

He dragged his gaze away from the window and gave the duvet cover one last tug to straighten it before his guest arrived.

Angel arrived later that day, all swirling black skirts, corseted velvet bodice and black lace parasol.

'Wow. Angel. Expecting rain?' He nodded at the parasol, even after she launched herself at him for an enthusiastic hug. 'And where's my cousin? I thought you two were joined at the hip these days.'

She pulled a face. 'No. It's my sunshade, idiot. And it's a bit hard to be joined at the hip when Kyle's still commuting back and forwards from Ontario. He had to go yesterday morning for his flight, and I hung around Taigh Fallon. I had some pieces I wanted to work on, so had a lov-er-ly day in my new workshop up there.' She grinned. 'And I came here, and I'll be heading home the day after tomorrow. But tonight, we celebrate. Because tomorrow we'll be picnicking on Ashaig beach, watching the sunset.'

'Ange, do we need to stay on the beach afterwards and watch it *rise*? Because isn't that technically the Solstice bit? The idea being you see the sun rise?'

'Well, yes. So that's why I've booked a pitch at the campsite. The tent's in the boot of the car.'

'You *what*? You *hate* camping!'

'Zachary, darling. As I *always* tell you, you need to be more spontaneous. Even *I* can manage camping for one very, very short night, just so we have the chance of seeing the sunrise on the Solstice.'

Zac opened and shut his mouth a couple of times. It was pointless arguing. It really was.

Good God.

So, because of the imminent horror of a potentially chilly night spent in a tent with Angel, and a horribly early morning – Zac knew the sky was destined to get lighter around 3 a.m., after it only got properly dark close to midnight, giving them approximately three hours of sleep – he was more determined than ever to have a decent night out in the pub and a good old sleep in his own bed the night before.

Once Angel had settled in, they headed off to Broadford, and the pair of them, as they always did, matched each other well in shots of whisky. Her ability to do that was always something which had impressed Zac about Angel, and tonight was no exception as they enjoyed rather too much Talisker nectar.

And then, with his inhibitions lowered and his mind pleasantly fuzzy, and the security of being with someone he could tell absolutely anything to, he said, 'Ivy makes the best cakes, you know.' His words, half-slurred, surprised even himself. He stared at the shot glass in his hand, stunned in some respects that the amber liquid had made him speak his thoughts out loud.

'Ivy? They must have been damn good if you remember them now.' Angel giggled, as if it was the funniest sentiment ever.

'Ivy is also an artist. She was going to do some lino printing, she said, and bring some more, some even *extra*, handmade things across to my shop. As well as making fudge and whisky cakes and shortbread.' He squinted at the glass again and shook his head, irritated somewhat by his hair, which he had suddenly realised was curling annoyingly somewhere between his chin and his shoulders and tickling his skin. 'She kept me stocked up. Because I used to forget.'

'And now you have to remember *yourself*. Poor Zac.' Angel reached over and patted his hand. 'God knows how you manage to run a business. But I have to say, your place is fine. Very fine indeed, even without Ivy. But you should have hung onto Ivy.'

Zac frowned and shook his head. 'I know. But then she got ensnared with the Hemp Monster—'

'Zac! Stop it! Poor man, you don't even *know* if he's a Hemp Monster!' Angel shrieked. Zac was vaguely aware that she was drawing a little bit of unwanted attention from the other clientele.

He decided to ignore the other clientele. 'Oh, he *is* a Hemp Monster. I'm sure he is.' Zac nodded sagely, then pointed at the door. 'And off she went … to be with *him* in Glastonbury. She was great for keeping the shelves filled.' He swigged the rest of his drink then made some excuse, changed the subject before heading over to the bar just to get away from Angel – because, even through the haze of whisky, he could see her sharp, dark eyes drilling into him thoughtfully, as she twisted her own shot glass between her fingers and looked as if she was going to say something terribly judgemental indeed.

In fact, he knew he was seriously in danger of drunk-texting Ivy, and that wouldn't do at all.

And he needed to do that out of sight of Angel, because even though it wasn't a good idea, he was probably going to do it anyway...

Meanwhile, in Glastonbury, the excitement over the Summer Solstice was overshadowed slightly by the fact that Ivy's Glasto Dream wasn't quite as dreamlike as she'd hoped it would be.

Gid had perhaps been a little sparing with the truth when he said it would be her studio space and her space alone. In actual fact, she shared it with a tarot reader, a mindfulness coach and, worst of all, another jewellery maker. A jewellery maker who had a much better footfall than she did. Morgana was situated right at the front of the shop, and Ivy was stuck at the back in the dark recesses of the building.

Ivy was still unsure as to whether Morgana was Morgana's real name. She didn't think it was, but wasn't about to ask her. Morgana could look pretty terrifying, and Ivy was still wondering if she sold so much of her stuff because she scared customers out of their wits when they walked in, glaring up at them from her dead, dark eyes. Morgana dressed to suit her name – so much so that Angel Tempest looked like a milkmaid in comparison. Morgana hailed from Pennsylvania, but Ivy thought Transylvania might be more her style.

But that was all an issue for another day.

She'd taken a six-month lease on a flat, and here she was two months into it, still finding her feet, still feeling her way, but still looking forward to celebrating the Summer Solstice somewhere so special.

'Gid, what do we do for the Summer Solstice around here?' she asked as the pair of them were relaxing on the grassy slopes of Glastonbury Tor in the long, drowsy hours after work with takeaway coffees and pre-wrapped sandwiches. It reminded her of that evening on the Cuillins with Zac, and she pushed the thought away before she began to dwell on it.

'Ummm – we climb this.' He patted the grass. 'Pretty obvs, eh?' He grinned. 'Great views. I took a sleeping bag up the other year. Very cool indeed. You don't have to spend too long in it, and it's a good atmosphere.'

'So ... is that it? We climb the Tor, and sit in a sleeping bag? Don't laugh, I'm genuinely curious!'

Gid really couldn't disguise his laughter and, despite the few misgivings she had about the way her Glasto Dream wasn't *quite* there yet, it made Ivy smile as well.

'Nah. There's more to it than that. Drumming, and chanting. Singing. Sexy pagan goddesses in flimsy clothes. And a Sun Salute. I did that last year. First time, though.' He lay down on the grass and, putting his hands behind his head, crossed his legs. 'Most exercise I've had for decades.'

'Well, it sounds brilliant. Will you come up the Tor with me tomorrow then?'

'Yeah, I guess. I've got two sleeping bags, but you have to provide the drinks. Just don't ask me to do the Winter Solstice with you. Too bloody cold.' He shivered and closed his eyes, effectively ending the conversation.

Ivy pulled his beard affectionately and he batted her hand away lazily, just as her mobile buzzed in her pocket. Taking it out and checking it, her heart thumped a little faster as she saw Zac's name on the screen. She opened the text and read it:

Happpy solsstc for tmrrwo. Angle here. Wish you wrw to

And that was it.

Typical Zac.

It made her smile, but instead of thumping a bit harder, her heart sank a little into her boots. Some people got drunk texts declaring undying love. It seemed that Zac's drunk texts were as vague as he was.

Have a good time with "Angle", she texted back. And leave off the bloody whisky, boy! You'll regret it in the morning!

She thought for a moment, then added two xx's at the end. Then she pressed send and bit her lip, trying not to imagine what Zac was doing to celebrate the Solstice on Skye; she decided to thoroughly appreciate what she was going to be doing here, in Glastonbury, to celebrate it instead.

Chapter Nine

Glastonbury, December

The months rolled around, and by December, circumstances dictated that Ivy had more or less decided that Zac's croft was possibly her favourite place on earth. If she closed her eyes really, really tightly, and thought about it she might actually be there, walking along the lane with that discreet sign made out of polished onyx at the end of it. Okay – maybe being blown along the lane with the winds coming off the sea, and then looking up to see the looming black shapes of the Cuillin Mountains as she walked along that path on the Isle of Skye.

So, was *Skye* her favourite place? She wasn't sure.

Surprisingly, and she never thought she would have admitted it, and as magical and beautiful as it was, Glastonbury didn't feel like home at all – even though she had now been here for eight months. It just lacked a certain something. And that certain something was a quiet, creative man with light brown hair that he always forgot to cut, the happiest, softest, darkest eyes she had ever seen, and a smile that could cut through the Scottish mists.

That man was Zac Fallon. And she thought she was missing him more than she had ever considered possible.

She attempted to unravel the thoughts buzzing around her head, to go back to the very beginning and to try and pinpoint where it had, quite categorically, gone wrong – the idea had always been that she'd come here to try and carve out a new life for herself; to set up her own little creative business, to have a little studio she could call her own, where she could sell her handmade jewellery and artwork.

She'd always thought that Glastonbury was the only place she'd ever want to be.

But Zac had changed all that. Once she'd begun to work for him, to get to know him properly, she understood now that the Glasto Dream had begun to fade into a pretty background; almost a watercolour wash over handmade paper, rather than the bright, gaudy primary-coloured canvas it had been for so long.

But she had insisted, to herself and to him, that she needed to do it.

For the umpteenth time a version of one of their conversations about it replayed in her head:

'What? Glastonbury? You mean it? You're going?'

'Aye. I am going, Zac. I've told you several times and I'm not changing my mind. Do I have to hand an official letter in? And how much notice do I have to give?'

'I don't want to accept your notice or your letter. I don't want you heading to Glasto …'

'Maybe it won't be forever, Zac. Maybe I just have to do this. Just to try it. I might yet come back.'

'Hmm. I'll miss you.'

'And I'll miss you. But we'll survive …'

She knew, she absolutely knew, that he'd had an odd look in his eyes, and she'd hoped so very much he'd argue more for her to stay; to tell her how he felt, not just leave it at "I'll miss you". But he hadn't. And if Zac couldn't express how he felt, if he couldn't just convince her that he wanted her to stay on Skye, she was definitely going to leave. After all, she still wasn't entirely sure if she'd been imagining his feelings towards her …

So here she was. Still in Glastonbury.

But he was still in Skye.

And that didn't feel very good either.

She turned over, unable to sleep, and her foot connected with the back of the sofa-bed. She pulled herself into a little ball, away from the edge, feeling pretty disloyal that she was thinking about Zac Fallon when she was in Gideon's home.

Because things really weren't great in Glasto for Ivy at that point in time, and that was part of the reason she was thinking more and more about Skye.

She pulled herself into a smaller ball. Christmas was coming, and she had given herself that deadline to decide what to do with herself. She'd been here since April, and the flat had been on a six-month lease.

The lease had expired two months ago, and now she'd moved in with Gideon while she tried to sort out her future. He'd offered her the tiny bedroom and said he'd bunk on the sofa bed. Ivy had argued and said it was only temporary, and there was no need to disrupt him for the amount of time she anticipated staying with him. She was looking for a new place, after all.

But truth be told, she couldn't afford to strike out on her own again.

She'd used almost all of her savings up and was yet to see a profit on her little business. Fortunately, Gid didn't seem in any hurry to kick her out, and he kept half-heartedly offering her the bedroom as time passed, but she knew that wasn't an option. If she got that, she would have no great impetus to sort her life out, and Gid would be stuck on the sofa bed for an indeterminate amount of time. She couldn't do that to him.

And she wasn't ready to admit to anyone that she had quite possibly made the biggest mistake of her life by coming here – the Glasto Dream had rapidly turned into a bit of a nightmare. Ivy screwed up her eyes as tight as she could and tried desperately to recapture the Island version of herself again; the Ivy who worked in Zac's friendly little tea room and who arranged the little bits and pieces of jewellery she sold from his shop, and the Ivy who teased Zac over the fact he had no clue about the meaning of the crystals she set so carefully into silver.

But then Gideon snored, and the noise travelled through the thin walls, and she could no longer hold onto her thoughts of Skye at all.

The Isle of Skye, December

This year, it was the turn of the derelict croft across the field to be covered in scaffolding. It was on Zac's land, and therefore his to do with as he chose – and Kyle, of all people, had chosen to be the one to restore it. He'd had the idea of converting it into a museum or a heritage centre and, as a property developer, he certainly knew what he was doing. Angel had insisted on putting a small Christmas tree up on the scaffolding, saying it was traditional and had to be done. Kyle and Angel had been over to Skye a week or so ago, and Angel had clambered up to the roofline of the low building, with a small fir tree tucked under her arm. She'd draped it in holly and threaded tiny, sparkling solar-powered lights through the branches.

'There you go,' she said, jumping down from the step-ladder, her heavy black biker boots landing soggily in the Skye mud. 'Almost perfect. We're just missing one thing.'

'And what's that?' Zac asked, standing back and looking at the decorations.

'An angel on the top of the tree?' Kyle grabbed Angel around the waist and lifted her up, swinging her towards the croft so her long black skirts trailed down and her legs kicked out helplessly.

'Stop it!' Angel wriggled around, laughing as he eventually put her down on the ground. He kept his arm around her waist though, Zac noticed. He hid a smile. They'd hated each other a few months ago, but life and love were funny like that, he supposed. The sparks that had flown between Kyle and Angel the first time they had met had clearly been born more of passion and wild, unacknowledged attraction, rather than an intense dislike of one another – not that either of them would have admitted that attraction at first. But they had done so eventually, and now it seemed unbelievable that they had ever existed without one another.

'No. It's not an angel you're missing.' Angel pointed at the tree and waved her hand around. 'Ivy. Ivy would make it perfect.'

'Ivy?' Zac had to stop himself from reacting at her name. He'd been thinking about Ivy more than was perhaps healthy, and Angel must have somehow known. He scowled and pushed his hair out of his eyes. It was too long again, but it would inevitably stay like that.

'Yes. Ivy. Some strands to thread through the branches with the holly. It would be pretty.' Angel was still looking at the tree. 'Traditional. You need traditional up here. For instance, I can't see my tree at home being popular on your scaffolding.'

'Black, fluffy and glittery.' Kyle nodded. 'With a Goth fairy on the top. Yeah. I guess it's not the sort of tree I grew up with in Canada.'

'Did you go and chop one down from a handy nearby forest, then?' Angel nudged him playfully.

'You could kinda say that,' he said with a grin. 'All covered in white snow. Not black sparkly … stuff.'

'Aye. I've seen Angel's tree.' Zac pulled a face, feeling a wee bit stupid that he had assumed everyone would feel the same cavernous Ivy-shaped space as he did. 'Pride of place in Goth Cottage.'

'Not this year.' Kyle grinned. 'We're having our first Taigh Fallon Christmas.' Zac was happy that Kyle had eventually bought him out, and knew that it had definitely been the right thing for both of them. Luckily for Kyle, Angel still loved Taigh Fallon. 'Goth Tree is in the lounge,' Kyle explained. 'We've got a proper tree in the hallway.'

'Only because you asked nicely.' Angel smiled up at him. 'And you got your way.'

'And thank you for that.' Kyle smiled back down at her and pulled her closer. 'Of course, Zac, you're invited if you want to come. Come over and stay for Hogmanay if you want. Angel's family are coming up for that.'

'Yes.' Angel nodded. 'The parents. Uncle Donald and Uncle Anthony. Jessie. And Rosa.'

'No thanks.' Zac's response was polite and perfunctory; as usual.

'I told you so.' Angel patted Kyle on the arm, then turned her attention to her best friend. 'I warned him that my sisters

88

were enough to put you off. Are you going to your parents again this year, Zac?'

'Nope. They're going to be in Edinburgh at my aunt's. They did ask me, but—' he shrugged '—not big on the mainland. You know me. And I did go last year.' He perked up briefly. 'I think they're coming here between Christmas and New Year though, so we'll have a second Christmas lunch.'

'You are so miserable!' Angel shook her head. 'You won't even leave the Island for *Christmas*.'

Zac was surprised. To him, it still seemed perfectly logical and nice to stay on Skye. There was plenty going on – lots of evenings with friends, a pub or three. A ceilidh, no doubt. What was the problem?

The problem, he had thought – and still did think, as he stared at the tree glimmering through the conservatory long after Angel and Kyle had left for the mainland – was that Ivy McFarlane wasn't here. And anywhere she wasn't was hardly going to be very festive, was it?

Chapter Ten

Ivy, bored of sitting at the back of the shop and not selling very much at all, decided to have a wander through the town and look at all the beautiful decorations in the shop windows. The Winter Solstice was creeping up on Glastonbury, and there was a sense of excitement and anticipation buzzing around the streets. One shop window displayed a rather fabulous corseted dress made of twigs and embellished with feathers and strings of crystals to resemble birds, and every business, it seemed, had decorations of some sort adorning their spaces: evergreens, and fairy lights and candles, twinkling and reflecting in the slushy puddles on the damp pavements.

Ivy paused outside a shop full of delectable Gothic treasures, which always reminded her of Angel. And, as ever, thoughts of Angel brought her thoughts around to Zac. She pushed her hands into her pockets and her fingers closed around her mobile phone.

It only took a moment of wrestling with her conscience before she pulled the phone out of her pocket and dialled Zac's number. Or, more precisely, the number of his little business – because that meant she wasn't ringing him *specifically*, didn't it? No need to feel nefarious at all.

'Hello?'

Zac's voice was sharp, distracted, and Ivy's heart bounced around her chest a little as she smiled into the handset. 'Might that be Zachary Fallon, owner of a particularly lovely jewellery workshop on the Isle of Skye? Because if it is, I've often told him how *not* to answer the phone.'

'It might be.' Suddenly, there was a smile in that soft, caramel voice. 'But I'm afraid he's a bit of a grumpy so and so, because he can't quite get this bloody brooch to look right, and his tea shop is not *quite* so lovely, means as he was left in the lurch some months ago by his invaluable and very best member of staff.'

'I'm sure your current member of staff can do a pretty good job.'

'She cannot. Not at all. Not at *all*. She's efficient, I'll give her that. But I don't know. She's not a keeper.'

'Is Effie not there any more then?' Ivy was surprised. As far as she knew, Effie was still there. Holding the fort. *Her* fort.

'Effie? No. She left to babysit her grandkids when their mum went back to work. I currently have a lady who feels it is rather beneath her to serve tea and coffee to the masses. And she hates dogs. Which doesn't bode well, as I'm now dog-friendly.'

'You personally? Or the tea room.'

'The tea room.' There was a smile in Zac's voice. 'I'm always friendly to dogs. Unless they growl at me, then I'm not so friendly.'

Ivy nodded, even though she knew he couldn't see her. 'I didn't know all of that. How long has it been since we talked?'

'Too long. And I always forget to tell you things in emails. So, I have to ask, to what do I owe this pleasure? You. Talking to me.'

'It's Christmas.' Ivy crossed her fingers. It wasn't a full-on lie. She did want to ask something about Christmas, but it wasn't the real reason she was calling him. She didn't know if she could admit the real reason to herself, if she was honest. 'I'm having a wander around the town—'

'—around Glasto?'

'Around Glasto,' confirmed Ivy.

'With the Hemp Monster?'

'No! Not with the Hemp Monster. Don't be daft.' Zac had conjured up this weird image of Gideon that he made more and more bizarre every time the man was mentioned. 'Why would I be ringing you if he was with me?'

'So you know who I mean then.'

'Of course I do. And no, I'm alone.' She took a deep breath. It really was a pathetic excuse to call him. 'I'm outside a shop that's full of Gothic things. I was going to get Angel her Christmas present and wanted your advice.' She had visited Angel, as promised, on her way to Glastonbury, and they were now firm friends.

'My advice?' Zac sounded surprised. 'I always send her jewellery. Nose studs. Or things for other piercings. Last time I saw her, she had an industrial sized bolt thing in her inner ear. She had her belly button done at uni.' He now sounded as if he was musing on his best friend's various piercings and trying mentally to count how many she had. 'Or things with skulls on. Earrings. Necklaces. Things. Aren't you giving her jewellery?' He suddenly seemed to realise he was talking to a fellow craftsman.

Ivy suddenly felt rather stupid. Of course that's what she would normally give as a gift! Time to think quickly.

'I wanted to get her something truly from Glastonbury. I mean—' she crossed her fingers again '—my stock is pretty much used up with the tourists and the fact we're coming up to Yule and the Solstice. And Christmas.'

'Ah.' Zac sounded a bit flat, and Ivy closed her eyes briefly. She hated lying to him but couldn't admit the truth. She was the one who had left and said how wonderful her new life would be in Somerset. And Glastonbury was wonderful, it truly was.

But Zac wasn't here. She opened her eyes and blinked away a quick, silly tear. He was so far away, and here she was, pretending all was grand, because he couldn't see it and couldn't challenge it.

As she tried to formulate some cheerful-sounding words, Ivy had a quick scan of the window and her gaze settled on an incense burner, depicting a dark angel resting on a tower with her dragon. She peered closer and saw that the way it was structured meant that the smoke from the incense would billow around the statue and, really, it was as good a gift as any for Angel – the figurine looked exactly like her. Currently, the figure had a tiny tinsel crown on her dark hair, but that was beside the point.

'It's okay, Zac. I've seen something she'd like.'

'What is it?'

'An incense burner thing. With a dark angel on it.'

'Ah. Yes, she'd go for that.' There was a brief silence. 'She's getting some ruby roses and silver skulls made into earrings from me. But she'll love your burner. It's good to hear business is doing well and you've sold so much. If you're out of stock, you're out of stock. That's great, aye?'

'Aye. Out of stock. And no time to make much more.'

'Sounds like it's going well for you, anyway. So – what do the locals get up to for the Solstice, then?'

'Ah! Well, that I'm still a wee bit unsure about. I believe the Tor is involved. And there's celebrations at the Chalice Well gardens. And Christmas trees in St John's Church from loads of different organisations. Which isn't really Yule or the Solstice, but I don't think it matters. Even the Druids put a tree in the display. Everything's just got a great vibe about it.' She looked around her and did feel a little Christmassy after that. 'It's lovely.' Then she forced a smile, knowing he'd hear it in her voice, even if she didn't entirely feel it in her heart. 'It's a shame you don't do the mainland. You could have come down.'

'No thanks.' There was an answering soft smile in his voice, but his answer was always the same. Thank God he'd never actually turned up at Glastonbury. She didn't quite know how she would hide the fact she was failing so badly at her dream. She hadn't even told him she'd had to move in with Gid – just that she'd changed address. 'But maybe one day I'll surprise you and turn up on your doorstep.' There was a bigger smile in his voice that time. They both knew it would never happen.

'Maybe you will. Look, I'd best go and get this angel before someone else nabs it. There are a few people in the shop and knowing my luck it'll go.'

'All right. Thanks for calling. I'm certain Angel will love the … angel.'

She laughed. 'That sounds so weird. You have a great Christmas, anyway, if we don't talk beforehand.'

'You too, Ivy. Oh – Angel put a tree up on our scaffolding on the old croft. It looks … different. I'll send you a photo.'

'You do that. It'll be good to see what the croft looks like now. It'll have changed a bit since I saw it.'

'Aye. It's got a roof now.'

His voice was warm – and maybe a little wistful – as they eventually bid each other farewell. But it was no use pining over Zac and Skye. Ivy had made her choice in April, and she had to perpetuate the myth that all was rosy. She pushed the door of the Gothic shop open and was immediately encompassed in warmth and soft music and the scent of incense. She could almost kick herself. Why wasn't she ecstatically happy in this marvellous town?

Because Zac was in Skye. And that was always the answer that came back to her.

Chapter Eleven

Zac had been fitting a polished gemstone into the centre of a Celtic brooch, his brow furrowed and a pencil tucked behind his ear as always, when she had called. All at once, the brooch had lost its appeal and his mind was hundreds of miles away, in a quirky town at the bottom end of England.

He remembered how excited Ivy had been to go to Glastonbury, and my God, he had suffered ever since.

'There hasn't been much footfall this afternoon,' came a loud, clipped voice from the doorway of his workshop, bringing him back to Skye with the proverbial bump. Judith, his tea room staff. Judith, who couldn't wait to chase the last customers out of the door and close up as early as possible. Sometimes Zac wondered why he still employed her, but the answer was simply because it was easier to keep her than go through the trauma of interviews and applications again.

God, he missed Ivy.

'No, it's blowing a hoolie out there.' Zac nodded towards the door where the wind was whipping dead leaves and twigs around the car park. When he had been outside earlier, he was sure he felt a few sharp flakes of snow tingling against his skin. It wouldn't surprise him if they did get some proper snow soon. 'But we can't assume nobody will turn up. People have cars and drive here, after all. They don't all walk. Put some Christmas music on. It'll cheer you up.' He knew it wouldn't. Judith hated Christmas music almost as much as she hated dogs.

Judith huffed and puffed and stomped away, grumbling

under her breath that it was a waste of resources to stay open for the next two hours. Zac yearned for Ivy's easy-going cheerfulness, and the hot coffee popped on his desk a couple of times a day as she came in for a chat between customers or did a little of her own crafting to keep him company. He was willing to bet she'd be singing along with the Christmas tunes if the place was empty – and quite probably even if the place was teeming with customers.

His eyes travelled over to the shelves where Ivy's work had been displayed so prettily. He loved to hear her talk about her gems and her artwork. Her lino printing was always something she was particularly enthusiastic about, and she'd talk about making cards and posters using the Scottish scenery as inspiration. One of their old conversations floated into his mind: *'The moors and the Cuillins and Eilean Donan. That kind of thing. Like old railway posters. With a twist.'* He remembered her leaning on the windowsill and looking out across to the ruined croft and the vast expanse of Skye behind it. *'Your croft there would look nice. I could do it in purples and greys and greens. Or a whole series of croft prints – in all the seasons. And!'* She had turned to face him. *'I could do sheep and wildlife. A set of four. Then people could mix and match. Pretty?'*

'Pretty.' He had nodded. But he was looking at her, and thinking more of Ivy's fair hair and green eyes than the Scottish scenery that framed her there.

'Good God.' He muttered to himself again and tried to concentrate on the Celtic brooch that was proving so difficult to work on. He put it down on his desk and walked away, over to the very same window he had imagined Ivy at. This was no good. No good at all. His shelves were looking sadly

Ivy-less, his life more so, and he wanted to see her. More than that, *needed* to see her.

The lights on Angel's tree twinkled and slowly a plan began to form. He owed Angel a visit to Whitby. He would, in fact, deliver her skull and rose earrings in person – and then, as he was halfway there already, why not pop into Glastonbury and surprise Ivy? Spontaneously, even. It would be a damn good surprise as neither one of them actually expected it to happen. Good grief, it was a surprise to *him*.

And, okay. Whitby was nowhere near bloody Glastonbury. But they were in the same country. Which was a start.

He stood straighter, still focused on the Christmas tree. If he could see how well she was doing without him, he might stop resenting the fact she was so far away and stop being so selfish. He needed to get over her, and what better way was there to do that than experience a few days in her heady, successful Other Life and see her there? See her happy. So he knew he was "onto a loser", as Kyle was fond of saying when he talked about various projects that weren't going that great.

New year, new start. Yes. He would do that. He'd go and see her, mope about her afterwards – over Christmas, no doubt, which wasn't ideal – then resolve not to miss her so much in the New Year. It was the only way.

The biggest problem was Judith – he'd have to leave his precious tea room in her care, which wasn't something he was excited about doing. Then the bell rang above the workshop door and two people came in, chattering excitedly.

'Ooh, let's see what we can get in the shop, and then we'll have a nice cuppa afterwards,' said a lady.

'Yes! I need a Christmas present for Fiona, so this will

be perfect,' replied the other. 'And I think a scone as well, perhaps? How lovely. It's so lucky we stumbled on this place. It's been a beautiful drive up, despite the weather!'

'Definitely!'

Zac grinned at the Christmas tree, before turning around to welcome his customers. If nobody interrupted his work, he could be quite genial and charming, really, despite how Ivy teased him about customer service.

And it was great that the tea room would get some business this afternoon as well. And even better that Judith had been very wrong about the fact that a bit of bad weather would stop anyone popping in and enjoying a pot of tea on Skye.

'There were some customers when you were taking your little break,' drawled Morgana in a bored voice as her eyes followed Ivy's track through the shop. Zara, the mindfulness coach, was away running a session at the Chalice Well, and Tallulah, the tarot reader, had a customer who was leaning eagerly over the velvet-covered table to see what the future had in store for her. 'I told them you had closed for the day, so they bought a ring from me. So sorry.'

Ivy knew Morgana wasn't sorry at all. She would have forced the poor people to part with cash whether they wanted to or not. She would have terrified them into it.

'Okay.' Ivy had long ago stopped saying "that's fine!". It wasn't really. It was plain rude. But she didn't want to engage Morgana in conversation. She put the incense burner on her own little counter and shed her coat.

Morgana gave a stifled little laugh. 'You bought that piece of trash? Seriously? Who the hell's gonna go for *that*?'

Morgana looked just the sort of person who would adore some "trash" like that – which made Ivy briefly question Morgana's "look". Perhaps she was like a chameleon who just dressed to suit whatever role she felt she needed to portray. With Angel, Ivy knew there was no ulterior motive. If Angel was a stick of rock, she'd have *Gothic Beauty at Heart* written all the way through her.

'A good friend of mine,' Ivy said, quite coldly for Ivy. 'I'm going to post it this afternoon. Now I must get back to work.'

Morgana stifled another laugh. 'Sure. You don't wanna let your stock get too low, do you?'

And that Ivy chose to ignore, despite the fact part of her wanted to punch Morgana right on the nose.

She looked at her phone and remembered Zac's lovely, lilting voice on the end of it not too long ago. Christmas was her deadline, she reminded herself. If business didn't pick up, and she was in the same situation at New Year, she'd leave. Give it all up as a bad job. She winced a little as she thought of Gid. She couldn't continue living down here in his home whatever happened. It simply wasn't fair on either of them.

And as if she'd conjured up the devil on her shoulder, the door flew open and Gid appeared, a roll-up cigarette dangling from his fingertips and a vague sort of look in his eyes. 'I'm wondering, Ivy, if we should bother with Christmas this year.' He waved his arm around the shop and nodded towards the street. 'I mean, it's like overkill, innit? The whole town. Can't bloody decide if it wants to celebrate Yuletide or Christmas.' He sighed heavily and threw himself down on the mindfulness coach's seat. 'I can't be doing with it. With the … *hassle*, man. You know?'

'Gid, I'm doing Christmas. And I'm doing the Solstice.

It's up to you what you do. But I doubt we'd get much of a tree up in the flat anyway. Now. Is there anything you *really* needed to talk about? I need to polish up some gems and make hearts.'

'To put them on leather thongs?' Gid frowned, suddenly the "Useful Friend to Have in Glastonbury" again. Not "The Guy She'd Made Use of to Stay Here". She blushed at the thought, but having said that, he'd never complained. 'Babe, it's not massively – a *single market* – here for heart gems on thongs. You get that, don't you? You need a USP. Unique Selling Point.'

Ivy felt her cheeks burn. 'Yes, Gid. But these aren't just *any* gems. Look.' She pushed a couple over to him.

'They look like cairngorm stones. Those Scottish things you like, yeah?' He pushed them back to her. 'Pretty. But not what people come here to buy. Your pictures are cool though.' He nodded to some cards and posters she had made in the run up to Christmas – intricate lino prints of the Tor and the Chalice Well and the Glastonbury Thorn tree; in short, Ivy's own quirky interpretations of the topography of the place. Glastonbury thrived on its folklore; the place abounded with tales of goddesses and fairy folk, and the layout of the town and surrounding areas was all said to reflect that. Wasn't the Tor linked with the Isle of Avalon from the Arthurian legends, and the outline of the Body of the Goddess seen in the hills and valleys, rising out of the flat Summerland meadows? Ivy had captured all of that in her artwork.

'Thanks. They aren't selling, though. Maybe it's too dark back here for people to see them.'

'Yeah.' Gid frowned and zoned out again, looking around him. 'Hey. Morgana. What's *your* secret?'

'Hey Gid. My secret is – my work is just—' she shrugged '—*great*. I guess. And unique.' There was a beat. 'You always used to think that, anyway. You gave me the USP talk a while back. Remember? When I first started out and pitched up down here? I kinda trusted you. Still do, I guess …' Her voice trailed away, then she glared at something she was working on and bent her head to it angrily.

'Yeah.' Gid's voice had a smile in it. 'Glad the pep talk worked for you. See, Ives, USP. *Got* to be a USP.'

But her stuff is still the first thing people bloody see! Ivy scowled down at her own gems, then pushed them aside. What was the point?

'So, we've agreed not to do Christmas then, yeah?' Gid stood up, bouncing between subjects, and looked around him again, as if he wasn't quite sure where he was or what he was doing here. He was vague in a very un-Zac way. Zac could make vague sexy. Gid just made it … annoying. Had he been so annoying at art college? Quite possibly, but he was always a decent friend.

'No, Gid. As I said, I'm celebrating Solstice and all sorts. I'm doing Christmas in more than just the traditional Christmas way. You can please yourself.'

'Hassle! It's just *hassle*!' muttered Gid, then wandered out of the shop, shaking his head and stopping to re-light his roll-up outside. Gid worked in a friend's mysticism shop. He also pierced body parts and did tattoos. He inhaled incense and all sorts of interesting things all day, so to see him out of his cosy little back-street comfort zone and on the High Street meant that even he'd had enough inhalation for the day.

Which was possibly why he was even more vague than usual.

Chapter Twelve

Angel hadn't been able to wait until Christmas to open her present, even though there were only a few days to go. She was in Whitby, closing up her jet jewellery workshop for the evening, finishing off her last few orders before heading up to Taigh Fallon with Kyle on the twenty-first – and wearing her new earrings.

'I adore them. I simply do.' She jiggled her head, so the skulls swung gruesomely from side to side.

Zac couldn't help but pull a face. 'I'm pleased you like them. They haunted me, those things. Aye. Every time I tried to sleep, I saw them winking at me.' He'd put little rubies in the skulls to make eyes and it looked very effective.

'But *I* think they're beautiful. Thank you.' Angel threw her arms around him and hugged him. 'You do know my taste. I've been chatting to Ivy, as well, you know. She was telling me all about the fun she's having in Glasto. It was probably just as well I posted her Christmas bracelet. I wanted to make sure she had it in time, because she's staying put. Her parents are at her brother's, and she said she wasn't joining them this year. She's obviously got enough down there to keep her occupied and it's an awfully long way to travel.' Angel sighed and gave her worktop a wipe down to get rid of the jet dust. 'Business must be good. I suppose there's such a lot going on there for the season.' Angel had enhanced her own surroundings with traditional-looking Victorian décor, and it complemented the esoteric little shop – once a two-up, two-down cottage on the cobbled streets of Whitby. 'I think I'll go down at some point for a festival. Not this year's Winter Solstice though – we'll be at Taigh Fallon and I've left it too late anyway, as it's only a couple of days away. Maybe we'll do it next year.'

Next year. The New Year. Zac wondered what resolutions he would have made come the New Year. Would he still be thinking about Ivy so much then? Or would he really have to swear off her and the very idea of her, if his crazy plan didn't pan out the way he hoped?

'She won't want us turning up down there if she's busy,' he said to Angel. And no, he wasn't even going to confess to his best friend what his nefarious plan was. The thought of what he intended to do actually made him go hot and cold all over. He wasn't that sort of person, generally.

'She's happy, I guess. That's the main thing.' Angel folded her cloth up and straightened some ornaments on the old mantlepiece. She had holly and ivy garlands draped across it, and a display of brightly coloured natural potpourri in a cauldron within the fireplace itself. The scent of orange and cinnamon and pine tickled Zac's nose pleasantly.

'Did she perhaps say if she intended coming up at all, any time soon?' Zac tried to sound nonchalant.

'She never mentioned it.' Angel swung around to face him and suddenly grinned. 'Zachary Fallon! Do you *miss* Ivy?' She nudged him painfully in the ribs. 'Because you've got that look about you. That half-crazed, half-dazed mooning look about you. Where you can't eat or sleep without her near you—'

'Shut up!' Zac elbowed her back. 'I'm eating and sleeping fine, thank you. All that *Wuthering Heights* blether might work for you and my cousin, but not for me. The only thing that's kept me awake recently are those bloody earrings.'

'But you didn't say if you *missed* her.' Angel emphasised the word again and laughed. 'Oh, Zac. Don't look so disapproving. I'm teasing. I *did* hope that you'd … actually. Never mind.' She busied herself with some more tidying, making a big show of checking things that were already labelled and displayed neatly.

'You hoped that I'd what?' He was intrigued now, despite himself.

Angel sighed. 'I hoped that you *could* perhaps see yourself with someone like Ivy.' She looked askance at him, curious, her perfectly arched eyebrows raised quizzically.

'I don't know.' He pushed his hair away from his forehead nervously. He'd had a fringe once. Now it was something which reached his chin on a bad day. And he had been hoping Angel hadn't been particularly perceptive this time in regards to Ivy and the fact he was missing her dreadfully. 'And anyway. Like I keep telling you, I don't suppose she'd be interested.'

'I just don't get your problem with it. Why ever not?'

'Because her life is in Glastonbury now. What would she want to do by coming back to Skye? Sitting in my tea room, serving customers drinks and snacks, when she can blaze a trail in Glasto?'

'Zac! You do realise the significance of those crystals she gave you, don't you? I *saw* the damn things!'

Zac's mind drifted back to Skye, even as he glared at Angel. He remembered one of the days that Ivy had been working companionably beside him, the mountains green and fresh out of the window behind him. She'd been sketching, talking to him enthusiastically once again about the intricacies of her lino prints. She'd had one eye on the courtyard outside, just in case anyone came in and needed some attention, and then she'd suddenly plunged her hand into her pocket and brought out a handful of sparkling gemstones. They nestled on her palm: one a shimmery, translucent pale pink; another berry-bright, vibrant red; and one a pale, smooth moss-green ...

'I meant to tell you,' she'd said, her cheeks colouring to match the pale pink. 'I had these left over from some work I did. Do you like them?'

He'd had to drag his eyes away from hers and force his attention to the jewels in her hand. He could have listened to her lilting tones all day, asked her all sorts of pertinent questions, and at the end still known nothing at all about lino printing. It would only have been to hear her voice.

'They're bonny. Very bonny.'

'Aren't they? They're all quite special as well. Look. This is rose quartz.' That was the pale pink one. 'This is rhodochrosite.' That was the berry-red one. 'And this is green aventurine.' She'd placed them in a line in front of him. 'Some people say they work best if you charge them on a windowsill in the full moon, but I think they understand a person anyway. Which one do you like the most? One of them might call to you more than the others.'

'I like them all.' He'd been surprised. 'Maybe the bright red one?'

'Truly?' Ivy had smiled. 'One day, I should tell you more about them. But that one is probably quite a good choice for you. Don't write off this one, though.' She'd picked up the pale pink one and took hold of his hand. There was, he could have sworn, another one of those little *zings* that shot up his arm and made all the hairs stand up on end. She dropped the crystal into his palm and folded his fingers over it. It seemed as if neither of them wanted to be the first to pull away. She had opened her mouth to say something else, and he had done the same at the exact same moment – then a 4x4 had crunched into the car park, and a family spilled out wanting attention, so the moment was lost.

The memories really didn't help him now, he had to say. And Angel was still looking angry.

'Of course not!' he snapped. 'I don't know anything about crystals. And don't forget she's from the mainland anyway.' He was on a roll. The more he thought about it, the more ridiculous it was. No. He'd just head home after this trip to Angel. Home to Skye. Away from all stupid thoughts of bursting into Ivy's workshop and going '*Surprise!*'—

'So bloody what?' cried Angel, startling him with the disbelief in her voice. Her very shouty voice. This was what you got on the mainland; shouty people like Angel Tempest. 'The *crystals*, Zac. I *know* she left them with you for a reason! *This* is what they mean.' She raised her hands and counted them off, her voice rising excitedly as she told him. 'Rose quartz invites love in. Rhodochrosite helps you learn to love yourself and teaches you that you're actually worthy of love. And green aventurine increases confidence and helps the owner attract new love and better finances! I saw them all last time I was up! You told me she'd given you them, and then you moved them onto the sodding windowsill!'

'Indoor voice, please, Miss Tempest. And so what? And how do you know all that anyway?' He threw the questions back to her, being, he was ashamed to realise, just as shouty.

'Because of where I work!' She sounded exasperated. And there was no sign of an indoor voice at all. 'Look around you! You can't be in my industry, in my town, in my *life*, without knowing a little bit about crystals.'

'You probably can,' he said, being deliberately awkward.

'Well, yes, you probably *can*—' she conceded snippily '— but my point is that *I'm* in the know and it was obvious that she liked you. She really liked you, Zac. And you!' It was Angel's turn to be on a roll now. She threw her hands in the air and shook her head, making the skulls wobble again, then pointed at him. Zac almost felt as if she was putting a curse on him. 'Zac. I despair of you at times. You let her *go*!'

'It was her decision to go! I didn't stop her. I couldn't stop her. If that was what she wanted to do, she had to do it.'

'She did. But did you try to give her a reason to reconsider?'

Zac thought hard. Had he? He didn't think he had done. 'I don't think so.'

'And then you wonder.' Angel sighed and shook her head. 'Right. I'm almost done here. I'll just text Kyle, then we can all go for a festive drink. And then you can come back to Goth Cottage and we can have a proper catch-up. If the cottage doesn't burst at the seams with three of us in there.' Angel's tiny home had been a fisherman's cottage once upon a time, and there was barely room to swing a hamster, never mind a cat, as Jessie had allegedly commented once, no doubt frowning at the lack of space for books. Rosa had apparently had palpitations at the doll-like proportions of the kitchen, and asked how anyone could ever be expected to bake anything decent in that sort of space. But Angel loved it and it suited her, and it was only for one night. Zac could tolerate an airbed in the attic room for one night.

And then – he felt slightly sick at the thought – he would head south-west to find Ivy.

But he wasn't going to admit that to Angel, regardless of how many festive drinks they had.

Next morning, after Angel had pressed a gift bag onto him and extracted promises of him visiting Taigh Fallon at some point over the Christmas holidays – to which Zac had mumbled assent he didn't really mean – he set off. And instead of turning north, he turned south and headed through the heart of England for almost six hours.

Which meant that at some point in the late afternoon, he ended up in Somerset. In Glastonbury. Of all places.

Zac's heart was thumping as he pulled up into a space in front of the ruined Abbey and switched the Range Rover off. He comforted himself with the crazy fact that he would have still had about three hours to go if he'd headed home to Skye instead – but then felt hot and cold at the thought of a twelve-hour drive home if this all went horribly wrong. Well – an hour to a motorway service station somewhere in Wiltshire that he'd had the foresight to book a room in for the night, and then another eleven hours tomorrow. *Ugh*.

What if, he suddenly thought, she wasn't actually here at all? What if she had decided on the spur of the moment to go somewhere else?

Zac wasn't particularly a spur of the moment person, so the fact that he was actually sitting here, in a car park, in Glastonbury, looking at the imposing ruins of Glastonbury Abbey was something of a shock to him.

'Bloody hell.' He sat back in the car seat and stared around him. There were people. People everywhere. Which wasn't surprising, as it was coming up to the Solstice, and people were here for that, weren't they? They'd be celebrating and chanting or whatever they did to celebrate and yes, it would be an extraordinary time of year. But Skye! He yearned for the wide, open spaces of the Island, the mountains he could see from his home, the Sound of Sleat not too far away from him.

A shiver of doubt ran up and down his shoulder blades as a family passed him, brandishing gift bags and laughing. This was a million miles removed from Skye. If Ivy was making a go of it down here, then what right did he have to slouch around the place and spoil it for her? Even if it was just a fleeting visit, as if he was allergic to people and crowds and would look as out of place as – well – as a Zac in Glasto.

'Good God.' Annoyed with himself, he pushed open the door and clambered out. He unfolded a piece of paper with two lines of writing on it.

The first was her address. He skimmed it, consigning it to memory, and then read the second line: the name of her shop. Okay. He could do this, he really could. He folded the paper up and tucked it in his pocket. He checked his watch. The shop. That was probably the best place to start, given the time. He hoped she wouldn't be too busy to see him. He had visions of himself creeping around the shadows trying to look inconspicuous so he didn't cramp her style by being too imposing and dour-looking for the customers.

Angel often told him he wasn't dour really, he was just quiet: '*And if people know you, you're anything but dour,*' she also said.

He knew that was the truth, to be fair. Most people did like him after all; once he let them in. But introspection wouldn't get him anywhere. Making his feet walk in the direction of Celtic Heart, Ivy's little shop, was the only way forward. So forward he went.

Chapter Thirteen

Ivy was straightening up her limited edition Solstice cards. She'd sold two today, which was two more than yesterday. Oh, and a silver Claddagh ring, which was good – but that was only because Morgana had nipped out to complain to the bakers that her lunchtime sandwich was soggy and hadn't been able to say loudly that "weren't Claddagh rings Irish and not Scottish? So, it was hardly a genuine Scottish piece of craftsmanship, was it?"

Morgana didn't get that just because Ivy was Scottish, it didn't mean that she was limited to selling thistle brooches. Not at all. To be honest, Ivy knew she really needed an online presence. Morgana had mentioned it on more than one occasion, and she knew the woman was right but didn't want to admit that fact. However, in the New Year, she would sort out an Etsy shop – she would—

'So – this is quite a nice place you've got here.'

The soft voice was as familiar to her as her own soul, and she snapped her head around to check she wasn't going completely crazy.

She wasn't.

'Zac!' She stared at him, quite frozen to the spot, her stomach suddenly feeling like a spin-dryer. He was, quite possibly, the only person she wanted to see in the entire world; but what made the spin-drying feel more like nausea, was the fact that he could now see what a rubbish little shop she had, and how dreadfully slow business was. He'd know, God he'd know how absolutely dreadful it all was. He would *know*. 'Wow. Zac.' She took a deep breath and forced a smile onto her face. 'This is a – surprise. Wow.' She thought quickly. 'You're lucky to have caught me. Gid was just in before, delivering some more of my workshop pieces to me – I'd almost sold out of Claddaghs, can you utterly *believe* it? But I couldn't nip home to get any because the place was jumping. So, he went and got me some stock, and well, yes, now I'm restocked and raring to go. But Zac! Honestly. It's wonderful. Wonderful to see you. Hug?'

'Oh. Ah. Sorry—' Zac looked stunned and, briefly, as sick as she felt.

Shit.

'Home? Gid went – home. And got your stuff from – home?'

'Aye, but …' She didn't quite know how to follow that one. Her stall definitely looked well-stocked. And it was clear that there wasn't really anywhere she could be making jewellery here.

'Oh. I knew you'd changed address, but I didn't realise you worked from … home. As well. With Gid.' He began to edge out of the shop. 'Great. Well. Fantastic to see you, the place is great. Aye.' He nodded and shoved his hands in his pockets. 'I'll let you get on with it …'

Ivy felt dreadful. Trying to make amends – because *God*, could she have made him feel any more unwanted or unwelcome? – she suddenly scurried around the front of her tiny counter and threw her arms around him. She couldn't help but close her eyes briefly as his arms came around her, a little hesitantly perhaps, and hugged her back. She inhaled deeply – he was the same as ever. His scent was unmistakably waxed jacket, the outdoors and something woody. She felt herself crumble as she realised he was here, he was actually *here*. In her shop. 'I never thought you'd ever, *ever* come this far south. What made you do it?'

'Ummm – I'd like to say you did, but that would be a bit corny. And a bit of a lie.' His voice was a little cagey as he drew away and looked down at her, but then his dark eyes warmed and a little half-smile appeared, ever so briefly. 'I was in the area, so it wasn't too much of a diversion to pop in. Aye. In the area.'

'Where were you? You never said the other day you'd be anywhere *near* me!' This was news to Ivy. She stared up at him, neither one of them moving their arms, so they were still in a kind of loose embrace. It felt good. More than good; it felt right, and she thought for one horrible moment that she'd start crying big, fat, girly tears at him and spill the secret that all was not as glorious as she had made it out to be. Then he eased her away from him and she really did want to cry then. 'You are a dark horse, Zac Fallon. You never said.' *But please,* please *take me back with you. Please!* She bit her lip hard to stop herself from saying that very phrase.

'Aye.' Zac shrugged, his eyes suddenly a little bit shifty. 'I had some stuff to deliver. To family. Cousins. In the area.'

'Really? You have cousins down here? Where?'

'Bristol. Aye. Bristol' He stuffed his hands in his pockets again. 'Might have taken a wrong turning when I left Bristol. So I just kept going.'

'Ha!' Suddenly Ivy burst out laughing. 'You amaze me, Zac. And I thought I knew you. But seriously – you came all the way from Bristol just to see me?' The spin-drying had, to be fair, subsided a bit, but her heart was now thudding around in her chest – she still couldn't get over the fact he was there, right in front of her. *Zac!*

'It's not too far. It's the same country after all.' He was deadpan. He appeared to relax a little, then his lips twitched at the corners. 'It's the only time I'm planning on being in England for a while, so I had to do it.' He shrugged again, then frowned. 'I had to. I'll be honest, Ivy. I needed to see for myself how you were getting on.' There was a beat. 'I think I miss you a bit. If you can miss a person who bullies you and shouts at you all day. Or maybe it's the coffees on tap I miss.'

'I did not bully you! I did nothing of the sort. I just told you to look up and smile if anyone came in. Potential customers don't know you've got a concentrating face which makes you look like you eat puppies for breakfast.'

'I have a face like *that*?'

He was genuinely surprised, and she laughed again. 'You absolutely do. But really. It is *so* good to see you. I can forgive you your crabbit face.'

'Crabbit? I look *that* grumpy then, do I? When I have customers?'

'You do. Look. Don't go. Would you like to see what I've been doing work-wise?' She touched his arm, just because he was next to her and just because she could, and then drew him to her counter. 'These are my latest lino prints.' She indicated the ones of the Tor and the Chalice Well. 'I've done some Christmas versions as well, in festive colours. See?'

Zac leaned in and nodded, thankfully appearing as if he wasn't going to run back off to Bristol after all. 'Beautiful. The ones you were going to do of my croft would look good in that style. And the ones of the mountains.'

'I might still do those.' She smiled. She could see the

Scottish scenery in her mind's eye, very clearly. 'And this is some jewellery I've been playing with. Like I say, Gid's brought more down for me – I was completely wiped out. Completely.' She stared at her stock, not looking at Zac, hoping he wouldn't spot any dust on the damn pieces. Because Zac didn't need to know it had taken her four months to shift one Claddagh. 'I'm lucky to have Gid on tap like that. He'd do anything for me. It's thanks to him I've made such a success of this little venture ...' She let the words trail away. It sounded so false even to her, that she didn't want to keep going and blurt out how rubbish it really was. And besides, even she was getting fed up of how awesome Gid and her bloody stock apparently were.

So instead, Ivy continued to show Zac the gemstones she'd been working on, and the polished stone hearts.

'They look a little like the ones from Skye,' Zac said softly, touching one gently.

'A little. These are different gemstones. They mean different things.' She didn't look at him for a reaction, but she knew what she meant. Her special ones had been left at Skye, in Zac's little shop. And yes, some of these *had* been brought with her. She just hadn't sold them.

But the really beautiful, special ones – no, she couldn't replicate them here, couldn't even bring herself to work with those gems at the minute. 'And then of course, I've got my Celtic Collection.' She barrelled on, indicating a display of Celtic knots fashioned into earrings and pendants, brooches and bracelets. 'Possibly my best sellers. After the lino prints. Like I say, the flat is overrun with silver wires. Gid has to step over them.' Again, that wasn't a lie about them being bestsellers. Zac didn't have to know there was a mere trickle of customers purchasing the prints, and a smaller dribble picking up Celtic silver pieces. And Gid had never had to step over any of her work in the flat at all. But it made her sound quite productive, she thought.

But dear Lord, she hated lying to Zac! She couldn't let him know it hadn't quite worked out as planned though, just yet. And she wished she could shut up about bloody Gid as well.

'It'll be a busy time of year for you.' Zac's mood seemed to deteriorate a little. He suddenly appeared a bit quiet and down. He nodded at the festive prints. 'I might have to buy a few of these to send to people. It'll thoroughly confuse them all, when they get a card with Glastonbury on it from me. They'll be shaking their heads over their Christmas dinners, debating on how that could possibly have happened.'

Ivy knew that was truth. She also knew it was good that Zac could poke fun at himself like that.

Then she saw a way of boosting his Christmas cheer a little. 'Are you calling in on Angel on your way back? I posted her present to her. Thanks for your help with that one – not.' She grinned and Zac perked up briefly. He smiled shyly and shrugged his shoulders. He knew, and she knew, he had been useless with that one. But he looked adorable, and she lost a little more of her heart to him.

'I'm sure I was quite helpful in some ways – I *meant* to be helpful, anyway. But no, I won't be calling in at Angel's. Once I've left this part of the world, which will be tomorrow, I won't be back for a while. I'm heading straight up the western side of the country to Skye. Are you intending heading up home yourself for Christmas?' His eyes lit up for a second and settled on her. 'The company would be nice, if you need a lift. I can take you with me?'

It was on the tip of her tongue to shriek *'Yes! Please, give me an hour to get my things together and I'll come with you!'* But she didn't.

'No,' she said instead. 'I'm staying put. I've got a few plans here, and it's too far to go just for a few days. Gid and I are just going to spend the day eating, drinking and making merry.' Her family lived on the mainland, quite close to the west coast of Scotland. She had grown up looking at the distant Island through her bedroom window and had determined to go there to live at some point. But then she'd travelled to Glastonbury as an art student, done a brief work placement there, and had always said she'd go back to the Somerset town to work properly. But it was different to how she remembered it last time; last time, she didn't know Zac, and Zac was what made the pull northwards stronger.

Zac regarded her steadily, and she felt her cheeks heating up. 'Too far?' he said. 'Well, maybe you're right. Especially if you've already made plans. I suppose I was a bit daft coming down here for a night. Never mind. If you change your mind, you can call me. I can be down to collect you in the morning.' He pulled a mock-pained expression. 'It's an hour to come for you, and an hour back to where I would have started, but I'm willing to do it for you. You like dogs, don't you?' And he leaned forwards, lowering his voice. 'And I like you better than I like Judith. My tea room would appreciate it.'

'I bet it would.' She suddenly found it hard to breathe, being so close to him, and took a step backwards. She didn't miss the flicker of disappointment that passed over his face as she did that, nor the fact he mirrored the movement and switched on another smile. 'So, how much are the cards? I'd like three, please.'

'Oh. The cards.' She told him the price and helped him select three. Then she put them in a little holly-berry patterned paper bag for him, and he smiled as he handed the money over. Their hands connected briefly and a tingle shot up her arm. Self-consciously, she folded her arms and stood awkwardly as he tucked the bag inside his waxed jacket to keep it safe. 'You might have missed the last posting date. And I don't believe you're so disorganised that you've left your card buying until today.' It was a trite thing to say, but it was the twentieth of December after all. Tomorrow was the Winter Solstice.

'I might have done, and I might be. But I like them anyway. Ummm – I don't suppose I can tempt you into a cup of tea before I go? It's a long drive for me, and if you've been rushed off your feet with customers all day...'

'Actually, that would be lovely. I—'

'Oh!' Morgana was suddenly there, in the doorway, clutching a replacement sandwich. She pulled herself up short, and stared at Zac, then glared at Ivy. 'Rushed off your feet? Sure.'

Ivy went hot and cold all over. She cursed under her breath and very much wanted to slap the woman. If it wasn't the season of goodwill and all that stuff, she really would have done.

'Come on, Zac.' Ivy decided not to grace the comment with a response. 'Tea would be lovely. I know a really cosy little café just along from the mysticism shop where Gid works. I might see if he wants a drink too. Let me just close up shop for now first, though.' She cast a quick glance at Morgana as she began packing up. The woman's mouth was shut in a tight little line. She looked very much as if she wanted to say something. And Ivy wasn't disappointed.

'Yeah,' muttered Morgana as they walked past her on the way out. 'If Gid comes here looking for you, I'll be *sure* to tell him where you are and who you're with. Just as well you're able to close up for a little bit though, isn't it? We can't *all* go off mid-shift.'

Chapter Fourteen

'What was that all about?' asked Zac as they walked out. Ivy led him to a little café up a side street that had holly wreaths decorating the door and a chalkboard on the pavement with a festive drawing on it, alongside a list of Christmas specials that were currently on the menu.

'Morgana hates me, basically.' They stood outside the café for a moment and Ivy screwed up her nose. It looked very kissable, but Zac pushed his hands further into his pockets and determinedly thought about *not* kissing her. 'Hey! Maybe she fancies Gid, and hates the fact I'm on the scene and we're going for a cuppa together. That's it. She's probably utterly besotted by him and hates the fact I live with him and she doesn't, and I get to go home to him every night and she goes home to, I don't know, a raven or an open coffin. Well, at least she doesn't have to put up with his snoring.' She suddenly grinned, but, despite the fact that Ivy's smile usually made Zac's world come alight, everything seemed a little chillier all of a sudden – *I'm on the scene. I live with him. I go home to him every night.* That wasn't good. That wasn't good at all. Ivy and Gideon's relationship must have blossomed quite a lot in the last eight months. He'd kind of got that impression from the succession of enthusiastic comments about her little business and how Gid was such a great person to have around.

Well, that turned everything on its head, didn't it? But why hadn't she told him that was the reason she'd changed her address? He thought, a little miserably, that maybe he didn't really know Ivy as well as he'd thought he did. Maybe he wasn't worth sharing that sort of information with, as far as she was concerned?

'So, he works just along here,' Ivy continued blithely. 'Give me a moment and I'll ask him if he wants to join us.'

'Oh – well. Yes. Obviously.' Zac cleared his throat and pushed his hands further down. Honestly, if he burrowed any deeper, his hands would come through the seams. Ivy smiled again and hurried away along the street, towards a black and purple painted shop with another board outside showing a very attractive dark-haired girl looking over her shoulder, a thorny trail of roses snaking down her spine. The model was wearing a Santa hat and the sign proclaimed that Christmas offers, Solstice Specials and gift vouchers were available. The model reminded Zac of Angel, and he wondered if he should maybe have confessed his intentions to her after all. She would have told him exactly what she thought, which would have been useful, as right at this minute, he felt way out of his depth with Ivy.

Look at her! She looked great, she had a successful little business down here, a home, a relationship – he shuddered at that one, not really wanting to believe it – and he had turned up to try and encourage her back to Skye. It gave him pause for thought. Because, of course, that was *exactly* what he had intended. How daft he was. And yes, pretty ashamed now he came to think of it.

Good grief.

Lost in his dreary thoughts, he stared gloomily along the road, wishing he hadn't come here at all. The icing on this particularly miserable Christmas cake would be the Hairy Hemp Monster loping out of the shop with Ivy and joining them. But it seemed he was in luck, at least in this case.

Ivy bounded out of the shop, still smiling. 'He's busy. Someone wants something pretty intricate on their arm, and he can't leave it. A dragon, apparently. So it'll take a while. It's just me and you. I hope that's okay?' There was an amused little note in her voice, and if he hadn't been conscious of her relationship with Gideon, it may even have sounded a little flirtatious. She took his arm. 'Do you want a tattoo while you're here? I'll ask him to do one half price. Of course, depending on how big it is, you might have to have a few sessions. So you'd have to come back. Or stay.'

He forced a smile on his face. 'No thanks. I'll leave the body art to Angel. She wears it well. It'll not be long before Kyle's sporting a tattoo. A thistle or something.'

'Or a Celtic cross. That would be quite nice.'

'If you say so. I don't really do pain, so if I ever got a tattoo, it would be tiny.'

'Mine isn't.' Her expression was guileless. 'It's pretty much covering my back now.'

'What?'

'I just keep getting bits added. It's addictive. I just ask Gid every so often and he draws a bit more in when we're watching TV on an evening in the flat.'

'Seriously? Our Angel has tattoo competition?' Zac stared at her, half in awe, half in shock. He'd never even thought about Ivy having one.

'No.' She shook her head and laughed. 'Not seriously. I've got a tiny one on my hip, my twenty-first birthday present to myself. It's not viewable to the general public.'

'Well.' Zac took a deep breath. He couldn't let her see how he felt that he'd just been punched in the stomach. Mission complete, and he'd only been here, what, half an hour? There was no way this girl was heading back to Skye with him, was there? How had he even thought she'd consider it? He was an eejit, well and truly. 'You learn something every day,' he said, with forced levity. 'So, what is it?' He made himself grin at her. He had to make the best of it, had to enjoy spending what little time they had together, because when would it ever happen again? The thought might have destroyed him, but he pushed it away purposefully. 'Some ivy? To match your name? Or a rose?'

'No.' She shook her head, then blushed. 'It's Tinkerbell. I loved her – there's something about naughty fairies that really appeals to me.'

'Hey, if that's what you like!' Zac took her hand. In a friendly fashion, of course, he told himself. 'Who is anyone to complain? Now – it's getting cold – shall we go in here? Despite the Hemp Monster missing out.'

'Hemp Monster.' Ivy shook her head in mock despair. 'Yes, let's go in. I can recommend the winter spiced tea and the matching muffins.'

They spent a pleasant hour or so in the café catching up. Zac tried his best to skirt around the issue of Gideon, instead drawing out information about the shop and the vibe around the town.

'You've probably come at one of the nicest times, to be honest.' Ivy was leaning towards him, cradling her mug of tea. 'Summer Solstice was wonderful, but I think this time of year has its own beauty. I spent Summer Solstice in a sleeping bag up the Tor. Imagine that!'

Zac couldn't disagree about the special beauty. The streets outside seemed to be buzzing with an energy he couldn't quite describe – something between an ancient form of magic and the usual Christmas spirit. Glastonbury was caught between two worlds; much as he felt he was at the moment. His inclination to shy away from the mainland conflicted with his feelings for Ivy. He knew now that if he had her with him, he would be quite happy to settle anywhere. His heart, he realised with a start, was clearly with her, despite the existence of Gid. That wasn't a good place to be in, but, realistically, what else could he do? There were fairy lights decorating the café, strings of them wound through shelves displaying vintage crockery and shabby chic. They reflected in Ivy's eyes, and he was mesmerised as she chatted about the Solstice celebrations they could expect.

'Hmm. I spent Summer Solstice in a tent on a campsite. All of two hours sleep I got with bloody Angel snoring her head off next to me.'

Ivy laughed. 'Yes. That was around about the time I got that interesting text from you. You and old "Angle".'

'Oh, don't! That was the whisky talking. I can't take any responsibility for it.' He smiled in return, feeling particularly ridiculous about that one, especially as she was probably with Gid the Magnificent in that damn sleeping bag – despite that, it felt comfortable being here with her, like they were cocooned in their own little bubble away from the rest of the world. But that was clearly not the best way to be feeling when you were, technically, on someone else's territory, with someone else's girlfriend—

And speak of the devil. Here he was – this person, striding in and looking around with arms covered in tattoos, a black T-shirt with the name of the mysticism shop emblazoned across the front and yes, more beard than Zac might have thought humanly possible on his typically good-looking face.

'Hey! Ives! My guy's having a break. The last scales on the dragon's tail touched a nerve, I think. Is this Zac? Pleasure to meet you.' The man was indeed Gideon.

'Gid!' Ivy waved at him. 'Yes, come and meet Zac. I'm just telling him about what's going on tomorrow.'

Gid slipped into the seat next to Ivy, stretching his black-denim clad legs out, and regarded Zac with half a smile on his face. 'Yeah. Solstice. Always totally amazing here.' He nodded and the smile deepened. 'Ives says she's looking forward to her first winter one in Glasto, yeah?' He slipped an arm along the back of Ivy's chair, and Zac's fingers clenched onto his mug. He had no right to feel so jealous.

'I loved the summer one. It was fun, wasn't it?' said Ivy.

'A lot of fun. So, Zac, are you staying for the celebrations?'

'Oh? What? Me? No – no, I don't think so. I've got a hotel booked about an hour away. I've only got it for one night. I'll be going home from there tomorrow.'

'Seems a shame to come all this way and be so close and not to join in.' Gid frowned and looked at Zac. 'You could have stayed with us, but I guess it's not the biggest of flats. And it's only got the one bedroom.' He cast a suddenly amused glance at Ivy. 'I guess the sofa isn't too practical, is it? Or *is* it?'

'Sofa bed.' Ivy's voice was ironic. 'It's comfy but, no, not practical to offer it to Zac.'

'It's okay.' Zac cut them off before he ended up invited over and camping on the floor, the sofa or in the bath tub. He was suddenly inwardly cringing anyway – they were *definitely* living together, which totally explained the change of address. *Good grief*. He was *so* stupid. 'Really. I've got things to do back home. It was just a flying visit. While I was in the area.'

He smiled at Ivy, whose face had fallen somewhere towards the floor. 'You weren't really in the area, though, were you? You made a special effort to come here, all the way from Bristol—' *Bristol? Bloody Bristol? Try Whitby!* he thought, his toes curling in sheer horror at his stupidity '— and I can't even ask you to stay in the spare room because there isn't one. Oh, Zac.' Now she looked as if she would cry. 'I wish ...'

'It's the season of wishes.' Zac looked at her. It might be disloyal to the Hemp Monster, but he desperately hoped whatever Ivy wished for would involve him – in a good way. 'I know I made mine a little while ago. It's not to say they always come true, though. But it's worth a shot.' He waved his arm around, encompassing the cosy café. 'If this town hasn't got gods and goddesses of all persuasions listening to people, then I don't know where has. Try it.'

'You're right.' The smile came back, just a little, but it was a start. 'Then in that case, my wish – my Christmas wish or my Solstice wish or somewhere-in-between wish – is that you come back tomorrow and you spend some time with me during daylight.' *Halle-bloody-lujah!* Zac fought back a very disloyal smile and waited for her to go on. 'I know it'll be the shortest day, and if I was any cleverer with my words I'd say something about it being a short day, so you wouldn't have to spend that much longer here because it's not a proper full day, if you think about daylight hours and stuff, kind of thing. But I'm not clever with my words, so the gist of it is that I really would absolutely love to see you tomorrow. If you could come back. I know it's a long way to drive ...' The words tumbled out of her mouth, and she looked a little shocked that she had even spoken them.

Gid had, Zac noticed, stretched over to a collection of business cards and leaflets on one of the vintage chalk-painted units. He didn't seem bothered. *He must feel pretty secure in that relationship then.*

'There's one way to settle this,' Gid said cheerfully. 'We're in one of the most magical places in the world. Let's see if Fate is playing nicely with us, yeah?' He tossed the papers over to Zac. 'Pick one of them. Call them. If they've a room free, you have to stay. It's meant to be.'

'Ummm ...' Zac was a little speechless. More than anything at this present moment – which was surprising, given his feelings for the mainland – and for Gid – he wanted to do exactly as Gid had suggested. But wouldn't that just be torture? If it worked, and there was a place available tonight, he'd have to see Ivy go home with Gideon and he'd be stuck in a random room alone knowing she was so close.

Knowing she was *so* close.

It was almost worth it, even just to know that.

He looked at her, took in her fair hair, the two long plaits that bounced on her shoulders as she moved her head. The eagerness in her green eyes as she leaned forward and smiled at him—

'Here,' she said. 'Stick a pin in the leaflets. Do it! Please! You know you have to.'

'Guys, this is *Glasto*.' Gid leaned forward too, almost as eagerly. 'Stuff happens, yeah?'

'*Och*, what have I got to lose?' Zac took a deep breath and closed his eyes. 'Go on. Do it.' His heart was pounding, almost willing Gid's supposed magic to be real. He heard shuffling as one of them moved the cards and leaflets around. It was Ivy, he guessed, a faint stirring in his nose of her perfume as the tiny, almost imperceptible breeze created by shifting papers around tickled his skin.

'There. Go on.' Ivy sounded excited and amused and, despite himself, he smiled.

'Okay. I don't have a pin, so here goes nothing.' He raised his forefinger and hovered over the table. 'This one.' He dropped his finger and touched a slightly rough textured card. Opening his eyes, he picked it up and studied the picture on the front. It was a pencil sketch of a cottage with ivy trailing around the door and he smiled again. 'The ivy's a good sign.'

'Very good. Go on!' Ivy, his Ivy, the real Ivy, was laughing, excitement bubbling in her eyes. 'Call them.'

Zac looked at her for a moment more, then shook his head with amusement. 'Fine. But I'm only trying this one.' He pulled his phone out of his pocket. 'You said yourself it's Winter Solstice. Everywhere is going to be busy. It's—oh! Hello. Aye. Umm. Right. You see, I'm after a room for the night, and I know it's short notice, so I get it if you're busy but …' He cast a glance at Ivy and simultaneously tried to take in what the lady on the end of the phone was saying. They had a room. One room. They'd had a cancellation, and she was happy to let him have it …

Zac could only nod dumbly, not taking his eyes from Ivy. 'Brilliant. Thank you. I'm just in … where are we?'

'Oh – the café?'

'Aye.'

'Right.' She told him the name, and he nodded and repeated the name to the lady – Ellen, apparently – as Gid rocked backwards and forwards on his seat, clapping silently and grinning through his ridiculous beard.

'Thanks. Yes. I'll check in a bit later if that's okay. I'm with a – friend – at the minute.' Ivy raised her eyebrows comically and he grinned. 'Yeah – I'll just get my card, and then you know I'm definitely coming. Aye, I'm not so far away, but we might …' His voice trailed away. He wasn't quite sure what he might be doing. Regardless, he fumbled his credit card out of his wallet and before he knew it, he had a room booked in Glastonbury in a house with ivy around the door.

This could either be a very good idea, or a very bad one.

Chapter Fifteen

Ivy couldn't have been more delighted. 'It's true, Gid. Glastonbury's magic is working!'

'It's all those wishes.' Gideon stood and stretched, then held his hand out to shake Zac's. 'Glad you got somewhere, mate. But, if you'll excuse me, I can't let the dragon guy wait any longer. He's wanting the Tor on it as well – dragon wrapped around its base or something.' He shook his head and wandered out, waving vaguely at them. 'See you at home, Ives, yeah?' And he was gone before Ivy had a chance to respond.

She leaned her elbows on the table, resting her chin in her cupped hands, ridiculously excited that Zac was going to be here tomorrow as well. 'You'll be here for the Solstice. That's so lovely.'

'And will you be on Skye for Christmas to make up for me having extra time on the mainland?' He mirrored her position, his dark eyes studying her. She knew he was teasing, but she still felt guilty.

'Zac …' She didn't know what to say. 'I can't promise that. Like I said—'

'Aye. Like you said, you have plans.' Zac sat back and smiled. 'No problem. I know you have a life beyond my tea room. So. I suppose I had better cancel my motorway room.'

'I suppose you had. I hope you don't lose your money.'

Zac pulled a face, getting his phone out again. 'No matter if I do. Some things are worth losing fifty quid over. And!'

He looked at her, a spark of amusement in those eyes, which made her unaccountably hot under the collar. 'Ellen gave me the room for half price. Said it was clearly meant to be that I rang her and took the room she'd prepared, so nobody had wasted their time. Imagine that.'

'This town is awesome.' Ivy clapped her hands. 'So, anyway, that was Gideon. Is he like you imagined?'

'Worse,' muttered Zac, typing into his phone. 'More beardy. More hempy—I can't call these people. It's all online. There. Done.' He put the phone down and sat back. 'I'm here for the Solstice, whether we like it or not.'

'I like it.' She smiled shyly at him. 'And don't be mean about Gid. It's thanks to him you've got your room for tonight.' *And I've got a roof over my head*, she thought – but she didn't say that out loud, of course. 'And I'm pleased you're here, I really am. I do miss you. I miss the tea room and the mountains and that little derelict croft. I love the sound of Angel putting a tree on it.'

'Kyle's got a lot of work ahead of him, but he'll get there. You need to see it. It's too hard to explain what he's doing with it.' The ramshackle building on Zac's land had been pretty much condemned, but Ivy knew Kyle wanted to renovate it properly, rebuilding it with as many of the original materials as he could. It was definitely a labour of love. No other project, Kyle said, had quite captured his imagination in such a way, in quite some time.

'Nice try. But I can't just drop everything and everybody and go to Skye.' She stood up and hoped Zac wouldn't notice how abruptly she had moved, even though she'd kept her voice upbeat. Anything, really, to get them off the potential opening-a-can-of-worms subject of Ivy's not-so-successful relocation 'Come on – I've got a business to get back to, and it's almost closing time, so I need to pack up properly. I'll take you back the scenic route. You can see the decorations.'

Hopefully, Zac would think she couldn't wait to get back because she may have lost a bit of trade while they were having winter spiced tea and muffins.

It was dark outside now and quite wet. It must have been raining, and when they walked along the paths, the lights shone into the puddles and the shop windows glowed warmly, the decorations as eclectic as the town itself. They were passing a window bedecked in silver and white, an angel right in the centre of the display and beyond that, there was a huge Christmas tree in the market place. And near that—

'What on *earth*?' Zac stopped outside a shop that had a model of a fox in the window, wearing a cloak and holding a staff.

Ivy laughed and decided she'd linger out here just a wee bit longer after all. What did it matter really? She'd rather be spending a few extra minutes with Zac anyway. 'It's Mr Fox. He's lovely! Look how Christmassy he is. Hey—' she nudged him playfully '—you haven't heard what you have to wear tomorrow. I'm going to take you to be kitted out right now. Look. There's a New Age shop just there. Perfect.'

'What? What exactly are we expected to do tomorrow?' Zac looked stunned. 'What do I have to wear?'

'I'm just joking. You can wear whatever you want, but try to put some white on if you can. And there's a couple of things I'd like to do, if that's okay? I'd like to climb the Tor for the celebration up there and then go with the procession down to the Chalice Well for their ceremony afterwards.'

Zac looked up at the Tor, darkly visible on the skyline. 'It's quite high.'

'Not as high as your Cuillins, and you don't complain about climbing those.'

'Very true.' Zac's smile was gentle. 'I managed to get you part of the way lassie, didn't I?'

'Yes, you did.' She remembered that fresh spring day when they'd taken the makeshift picnic to the base of the Cuillins. It had been damn near perfect.

Ivy, with some effort, dragged her mind and the conversation back to the present day. 'And tomorrow, at daybreak, it's supposed to be like the sun rolls up the hillside and balances on top of that tower up there. But I'm not going to drag you up there for sunrise. Have no fear. We'll do the main part of the ceremony at a more civilised hour. You've had a long drive today and you'll need your sleep.'

'If I'd got here earlier, or could stay for longer, I might have considered it. It would have been good to see if it was true.' Zac looked up at the sky and the thick clouds. 'I'd say we're in for snow, though. Once the temperature drops, this rain will disappear and turn into snow.'

'I love your ancient weather wisdom.'

'Never lets me down.'

They stood in front of the big tree, the flickering lights shining multi-coloured jewels on Zac's hair. Ironically, he seemed perfect for Glastonbury. He was part of it, he was right here; yet he seemed to exist outside of the real world. He, like her, was simply passing through.

'Are you cold? Here, let me.'

Ivy blinked, taken aback as Zac unwound the tartan scarf from around his neck and placed it around hers. She realised she had been shivering. But she wasn't cold. There was a strange sort of energy that was creeping around her, and she thought that it had a lot to do with Zac being so close. He was *here*! It still didn't seem quite real. Even if she'd been a wrong-direction diversion from Bristol.

'I'm sure you need it more than I do,' she managed, conscious of his hands so close to her skin. Accidentally, or maybe not accidentally at all, his fingers brushed her neck, lifting the end of one of her plaits to fit the scarf underneath, and she thought she might ignite on the spot in a display to rival the Christmas lights of Glastonbury. 'You're from the north, after all. You'll need your scarf for Skye.'

'Yes. I will. But, for now, I'm down south, and you're shivering.' She could feel his warm breath on her face, a lingering scent of spiced tea clinging to him, and she wondered what would happen if she collapsed in a gibbering wreck on the ground beneath the Christmas tree in the market place. Whether someone would eventually come and scrape her up, or whether she'd be left in a crumpled, Christmas-themed heap, pining after Zac for the rest of her days.

'It's a shame you missed the Glastonbury Frost Fayre,' she managed to burble. 'That was last month. You should have come.'

'Hmm? Maybe.' He was tweaking the edges of the scarf now, then he smoothed the thing down and put his hands in his pockets, almost guiltily. 'Wouldn't have been in the area then. I shouldn't really be here now.'

'But it's nice you're here. It's very nice.'

'Just nice?' He looked at her, slightly sadly it seemed, then straightened up. An almost imperceptible barrier came down in his eyes. 'Your hairy friend has a lot to answer for.'

'Gid? But what—?' She was confused. Yes, she was here because of him, but it didn't mean she had to stay, did it? Her barriers were crumbling brick by gemstone brick, and she was just about to say something to that effect when there was a ringing sound, and they both jumped.

Zac stared down at his pocket and pulled his phone out. 'Angel? Hey. What's up, hen?'

Ivy heard an indignant squawk, as Angel presumably picked up on the word "hen". She had told Ivy that Zac had used that term of endearment once and once only on her, and he had been very, very distracted at the time. It was, Ivy recalled, just after he discovered he'd inherited the house from his great aunt. She buried her chin in his scarf, inhaled his scent and half-wondered, half-hoped that she'd been the one to distract him this time.

'No. No, I didn't call you when I got home, because I'm not home yet. I'm nowhere near home yet. No. I didn't decide to stay over in Scotland on the way. I might have taken a diversion. Do I have to report all my movements to you? I do? I *do*! I see.' He looked at Ivy and pulled a comical face. Ivy, despite herself, burst out laughing. The squawk came again, louder this time, and Zac closed his eyes, turning his face heavenwards and shaking his head in mock despair. 'Yes, Ange. Yes. I'm with someone. No. No, I don't think it's any of your business who it is.' He looked at Ivy and winked. He was enjoying winding Angel up, and Ivy laughed again. She wondered briefly if she'd imagined that electricity between them a few moments before. Whatever undercurrents had been there had fizzled that particular energy away, and she and Zac were, seemingly, back to being friends and enjoying one another's company easily.

Shaking her own head, she held out her hand and Zac, grinning, passed the phone to her. 'Hey Angel. How's things?'

'Ivy? Ivy! Oh my God, he found you on the way, did he? Are you home for Christmas after all? That's brilliant. Look, we're having a bit of a do at Taigh Fallon. Could you make it, do you think?' Angel knew where Ivy's family home was, and obviously it made sense for her to think Ivy was there. 'We're actually heading there tomorrow. It's all a bit more spontaneous than we'd planned, but I can't wait to go and we already asked Zac, but you know what he's like. Maybe you can convince him if you're home.'

'No. No, I'm not home. And, actually, Zac's in Glastonbury. With me. He's here for the Solstice.'

There was a deathly silence on the end of the phone, followed by an ear-splitting whoop of joy. 'In Glastonbury? He's *there*?' Her voice bellowed down the phone, making Ivy hold the hand-set well away from her ear. 'You dark horse, Zachary Fallon. You – you – Christmas *imp*! Why didn't you *say*?'

'You're a Christmas imp, apparently,' Ivy told Zac dryly.

'I heard.'

'I never knew there was such a thing as a Christmas imp.'

'Me neither.'

Angel bellowed down the phone again. 'Well, let me take the opportunity to thank you for my gift, Ivy! It's beautiful. Soooo beautiful.'

'Oh! I'm glad you got it. Great.'

'Yours is in the post. It should be with you soon.'

'I'll look out for it. Do you want to speak to Zac again?'

'Do I *want* to speak to him? No. Do I *need* to speak to him, though? Yes. Yes, I do, to find out exactly why he took such a mahoosive diversion.'

'He came to Bristol. I'm not that far from Bristol.'

'Bristol? Why did he go to *Bristol*?'

Ivy flicked a glance at Zac. 'He has cousins ...'

'*Cousins*? Okay. That's a new one on me. Must be a weird branch of the family tree. Whatever. If he said so. Christmas does weird things to people,' said Angel sagely. 'It makes you want to *be* with people. And Zac is so lovely, he would want to be with the right person at exactly the right time. I'd absolutely trust him with my life. Or my heart, if my desires lay thus and they absolutely do not and never have done. He needs that very special person in his life, I've always said that. Okay. Let me speak to him.'

'Sure. Merry Christmas, Angel.' Ivy was still reeling a little at Angel's confusingly long speech. What on earth was she implying? Actually, she had a good idea what she was implying, but that was really nothing she had a right to expect from her friend and ex-employer ...

'And to you,' Angel replied super-warmly.

Ivy handed the phone back to Zac, who was still dappled with fairy lights. But now there were more – there were sparkles in his hair, and Ivy realised it had started to snow.

How utterly magical this evening was turning out to be.

After he had fended off Angel's inquisition, with some well-placed mutterings and some nicely side-stepped questions, Zac stuffed his phone back in his pocket.

'Interesting conversation,' he said and frowned. 'When I could get a word in edgeways. She's my best friend, and

I would have texted her later. I would have said I was safe. Having said that—' he grinned '—I might not have said where I actually was, because then I would have had to face *that* conversation. Sorry. I didn't tell her I was going to Bristol. I'm in trouble.' *What was one more Bristol-based fib?* he reasoned to himself.

'It's fine. Anyway, I'm pleased you're not going to that motorway place now. Look – the snow's getting heavier.'

'It is. And at least I don't need to drive far in it. That's braw.'

'Very braw. Very good indeed.' Ivy nodded. 'And it's maybe a good chance for you to go and get your car and find your bed and breakfast before it settles on the roads.' There was a beat and her cheeks flushed a little pinker and his heart melted a little more. 'Will I see you later? You could come to the flat or—'

'No.' He answered, maybe too quickly. 'I won't come to the flat. I'm sure Gid won't want me hanging around. I might just find a pub and see how it goes. It's a shame to spend the night alone.' His own face heated up. 'I didn't mean that the way it sounded.'

'That's fine. Don't worry. Look.' She stood up straighter and took a step towards him and, suddenly, she was so very close. 'There's a really nice pub along there.' She pointed along one of the roads. 'I can maybe meet you? Eight o'clock or so? I think they've got live music on tonight. It's not quite a ceilidh, but it's fun.'

'That does sound fun. Will Gid be okay with it?'

'Of course he will. I have my own key, you know?' She smiled at him and he forced one back.

'I'll see you there then. I'm parked over by the Abbey. I'll walk you back to your shop, and then pick up the car. Then I'll get myself sorted and come to the pub.'

'Excellent.' She nodded, and there was an awkward moment when Zac felt as though he should perhaps kiss her. He settled for an even more awkward peck on the cheek and a hug. 'I'm pleased I took a diversion today.'

'Me too.' And she tucked her arm into his, in a very friendly, platonic way, and together they headed through the snowy streets to Celtic Heart.

It was a very pleasant evening. Ivy made a special effort getting dressed to go out. It was maybe a little ridiculous – it was only Zac, for heaven's sake – but she felt as if the occasion demanded it.

Ivy was a Highlands girl, and usually spent her winters dressed appropriately – which meant lots of layers and warm clothing. She did have one particular dress that she was very fond of, however, and it was this one that she put on tonight. It was knee-length, dark green velvet, closely fitted, with long emerald chiffon sleeves. She teamed it with a pair of boots, as she was still practical and it was still snowing lightly. But she made an effort with her make-up and even got the flicky eyeliner perfect. A slick of sugar-pink lipstick, a few well-placed curls created with her straighteners, and she was good to go.

'Going somewhere nice? With someone nice?' Gid was sprawled on the chair, messing with an iPad, and he looked up at her as she clambered over his legs to reach her handbag.

'Yes thanks. There's live music on at the King William. I'm going there for a wee while with Zac.'

'You're dressed very particularly, young lady.' Gid grinned. 'Don't think I've seen that frock before.'

'You won't have done. I've never had cause to wear it. See you later?'

'Yeah. I'm not going anywhere. Just chilling.' He waved his hand in a *laissez-faire* manner and lolled a little more. He was obviously going to enjoy his evening on his own, in his own flat. Ivy couldn't blame him really.

'I'm sorry I'm still here, Gid. I know it isn't easy for you.'

'You're less bother than a dog,' Gid commented. 'You can at least take yourself out and you've sometimes got conversation.' He shrugged.

Ivy laughed. 'Thanks, I think. I'll see you later.'

'Don't hurry back.' He smiled. 'I'm assuming his accommodation will be fitting, if deemed necessary?' He waggled his eyebrows questioningly, and she shook her head.

'I will be coming back here. I'm not going to jump into bed with him. God, he's my ex-boss.'

'You look very nice for a casual evening with your ex-boss. And anyway, I meant in case you got snowed in at the pub and had to fight your way back to a wee warming hearth for a wee warming dram.' His fake Scottish accent was appalling.

Ivy tossed a newspaper at his head and he ducked out of the way. 'Enough already. He's travelled a long way to see me. I want to look good for myself, for my own self-image, and also to ensure he's not in the company of a rag-bag.'

'Yeah, yeah. You could never be a rag-bag, but I get it. Okay. See you later. Enjoy.' He went back to his iPad, and Ivy shook her head. She knew his Pinterest habit was almost as bad as hers. He'd be looking at tattoo designs and random piercings, thinking about adding to his own, no doubt. But at least tonight he could do it in peace.

'See you, Gid.' She grabbed her bag and hurried out of the tiny flat, almost running to the pub. It was going to be so good to spend this evening and part of tomorrow with Zac. It was her secret Christmas wish come true.

Chapter Sixteen

Once Ivy got to the pub, she walked in and a wall of heat and laughter assailed her. She scanned the crowds a little nervously. The place was jumping and the band were setting up. She spotted Zac was sitting at a table in the corner, looking around him in awe, nursing a pint of something. He usually opted for whisky at home, so it was quite a surprise to see him with an ale in front of him. He spotted her and stood up quickly, waving at her.

'Zac!' She hurried over to him, and he embraced her in a warm, Zac-smelling hug. She closed her eyes briefly. It was lovely. 'It's going to get busy, I think. Lucky you found a table.'

He nodded, drawing away from her and indicating that she should sit down opposite him. 'You could be right. I thought we had the monopoly on this sort of social gathering up on the Island, but it seems I'm wrong. You look grand, by the way.'

Ivy smiled. It was enormous praise, *grand*, coming from Zac. 'Thanks. I thought I'd make an effort.'

'I thought I'd do the same.' He smiled that dazzling smile she adored so much. 'See, I chose a different drink. That's how special this occasion is.'

'Well, I'm honoured. You look very nice too.'

'I wasn't sure what to wear, so thought I couldn't go wrong in this.' He was wearing pale-coloured trousers, an open-necked grey shirt and a diamond-patterned V-neck sweater on the top. His waxed jacket was tossed onto the seat next to him along with his tartan scarf she'd given back before she'd left him before. He'd brushed his hair and it framed his handsome face perfectly. The way the light shone from the wall lamps highlighted his cheekbones, and Ivy had to tear her gaze away from him. He did fit in, as there was a joyously eclectic collection of clientele there, and whatever you wore would fit in, but his soft Scottish voice and his distinctive aftershave took her straight back to a wild moorside on Skye.

'You haven't gone wrong. Not at all.'

'Good. Now, what would you like to drink? Probably policy to get settled before the music starts.'

'I think so.'

It was small talk of the smallest degree – but it was nice. It was comfortable and relaxed, and Ivy didn't have to pretend to be anything she wasn't, apart from a successful creative artist, of course. But even that was incidental. Once they'd covered the styles of jewellery they were both producing, talked about Ivy's lino prints, shared tales of various customers and co-workers and compared Judith and Morgana's customer service skills, the music was in full flow and Zac was leaning on the table, his chin in his cupped hands and his eyes, slightly hazy from the real ale, fixed on Ivy.

'This is so nice. I like Glasto,' he said. 'I like it with you, Ivy McFarlane. And I like it near Christmas. And I like the snow and I will like the Solstice – stuff – we're doing in the morn. But I think most of my heart is still in Skye.'

'Most of it?' She mirrored his pose, sitting almost exactly as they had been in the café over spiced tea. But here, with no Gid and no thoughts of returning to Morgana's lair, she could allow herself to fully drown in his eyes. The music was still playing, and she heard the first bars of a traditional

Christmas song start up. The event was winding down, and the high-energy, toe-tapping music was melting away into some of the Big Band Christmas tunes from the 1940s and 50s.

'Aye.' He sighed. 'There are little bits left on the mainland here and there.'

'Here and there?'

'Aye. Like in Whitby. Because Angel is my best friend, so she gets a part. But there are bigger parts elsewhere.'

It was more what he didn't say, more what his eyes said, that had her face heating up like a flame had scorched her cheeks. Then he sat back and threw her completely. 'My family. They have a big part of my heart. The Bristol lot, especially. Would you like to dance?'

'Dance?' The question took her by surprise, and she sat up, feeling rather stupid. She'd sort of hoped that the journey to Glastonbury had been a little more spontaneous than an afterthought to a family visit – especially after what Angel had said. But she guessed she was wrong.

But hold on. Wait a moment – she grew hot and cold all over, and almost felt herself shrink back into her green frock just a little bit. Perhaps Angel was right to be suspicious over the Bristol cousins. Maybe he genuinely didn't have any. Maybe, horror of horrors, it was a woman he was visiting?

'Aye. Look. They're getting up. It's hardly a ceilidh, but I'm sure we can manage.'

'I'm sure we can.' She swallowed the horror of that last thought, drained the last of her mulled wine, and forced a smile. *Friends*. That's all they were. All they'd ever be.

Zac stood up and held his hand out to her. She took it, and again there was that fizzing, tingly sensation that took her breath away. Did friends *really* have that effect on other friends? *Good grief.*

Quashing the feeling, she allowed Zac to lead her into the crowd of people who had decided to dance. He put his arm around her waist and pulled her closer, and after a slightly awkward moment where she forgot where her hands should go, they were, surprisingly, carried away with it all, laughing and spinning around the dance floor. The clientele were even joining in with singing some of the better-known tunes like 'Silver Bells' and 'Winter Wonderland'. It was a mad, yet completely relaxed, feel-good half hour or so.

Of course, that feeling made it all the more difficult to say goodbye to him when they were standing in front of the Christmas tree again, the freshly-fallen snow covering the footprints on the pathways, the last bars of 'Have Yourself a Merry Little Christmas' still whirling around her head.

'That was a lot of fun, but I guess it's time to walk you back home now,' Zac said. 'Especially if you've had a busy day being fabulous and selling things. I should have thought about it more before I came down and we ended up in a pub. I'm on holiday. You're not. Sorry about that – I'm selfish, aren't I?' His eyes were warm and heavy, drilling into hers, a mischievous smile hovering around his lips; all because of the ale, no doubt.

He was definitely a little more dishevelled than he had been at the beginning of the evening, but it was a good dishevelled, and Ivy's heart thudded again as she looked at him. 'Zac—'

It was on the tip of her tongue to put him right, but even as he looked at her curiously, his eyebrows raised, she forced herself not to offload onto him. It was unfair, and *come on*! She was Ivy McFarlane and couldn't ever admit defeat. He seemed so happy for her – so supportive, and pleased she'd done so well. So, instead she forced a smile onto her own lips. 'Come on, Zac. I always like visiting pubs with you – you know that very well.'

'Aye, but the pubs we used to go to on Skye had proper ceilidhs, didn't they?' He grinned. 'Remember that one where you fell over when we were doing the Hooligan's Jig?'

'Oh! Yes! That was a bloody dangerous night – how on earth could you let me drink so much whisky, Zac Fallon? And I only *nearly* fell over because you picked me up and swung me round too hard!' She couldn't help but laugh, remembering it.

'We were enjoying ourselves. That's what happens.' He looked down at her for a moment, the smile wavering a little on his face. 'We had some good times. I do miss you.'

'I miss you too. And we did have some good times, didn't we?'

'Aye. But now, I have to get you home.' His voice was suddenly decisive, and she realised their hands were intertwined. Zac must have realised as well, because he suddenly let go of hers and his arms dropped awkwardly by his side.

'Oh, there's no need to walk me home, Honestly. *Pretty* sure I can find my way. I'm not half as drunk as I was that ceilidh night ...' She attempted an airy response, but inside her heart was pounding. If he walked her to Gid's, then she would feel even worse at saying goodbye to him on the doorstep. Gid could be contorted in any position possible by now, quite probably snoring his head off, and she couldn't ask Zac in, she just couldn't—

Zac looked at her and held her gaze for a few moments

that seemed like a lifetime. His eyes darkened, the smile slipped off his face and before she knew it, she was tilting her head up to his …

'Are you *sure* you're not drunk?' he asked, his voice low, sending mad little shivers of anticipation through her body. 'Because I think I am. And I think I've been wanting to do this since I got here—'

Suddenly, his warm lips were on hers, burning a trail of fire right down to her toes. His hands were on her shoulders, holding her tightly; then, just as quickly, he pulled away. 'God. I'm sorry, Ivy. Really. It's just – you know. Christmas. Solstice. Whatever.' He pushed his hand through his hair. The careful sort-of-style he had managed to create at the beginning of the evening had become messy and tousled at some point, and now it was mussed up even more. 'Wow. I truly am sorry. I'll take you home now. Back to your Gideon.'

'No!' Her response was hurried. She was pretty sure she must look as shocked as she felt. How could a kiss do that to her? Her lips were tingling, desperate for more. 'I'll just get a taxi. Really. It's easier. Look – there's one now.' Quickly, Ivy turned and flagged the passing vehicle down. 'I'll … see you tomorrow. If you still want to? Up on the Tor? For eleven?'

'Eleven?' Zac looked a little thrown and a little lost, but he smiled, slightly sadly, and shrugged. 'Well – I would still like to go – but do *you*? I mean …' He let the words trail away, and Ivy felt her face flush. More than anything, she wanted to meet him tomorrow – well, apart from the fact that she didn't want this actual evening to end, and getting in a taxi and driving away from Zac was the very *last* thing she wanted to do. But what choice did she have? If she went back to his B&B … no. She couldn't. She climbed into the car and looked up at him. 'We need to be there from quarter to, to climb to the top.'

'Quarter to. Great. I'll see you at the bottom. Thank you for tonight.' He smiled briefly, and Ivy found herself in the taxi, with it moving away and Zac standing shivering beneath the Christmas tree. Then she blinked and he was gone, disappearing into the shadows.

The taxi rolled past a group of revellers, but one person was standing to the side of them, all dressed in black and looking as if she didn't belong. It looked a lot like Morgana, but Ivy had very little sympathy to spare that woman in general, and even less tonight when she had more upsetting things to think about – like how, at the end of such an amazing evening, it seemed like she couldn't allow herself to tell the one person she thought she could trust how things really were; and how he had just been standing there, watching her leave.

And what on earth did he mean by "your Gideon"? Was he no longer the Hairy Hemp Monster? Had Zac finally accepted that Gid was just … Gid? And not a demon who had dragged her away from Skye for his own nefarious purposes? She hoped so. She really hoped so, because she'd love it if the two of them could actually get on properly. If she felt like she didn't have to constantly defend her friend to Zac, it would make things a lot easier. Silly as it was, she *did* feel torn between the two of them. Torn between her life down here and her life on Skye.

But it was only as she was letting herself in to the flat, with the sound of Gideon's snoring alerting her to the fact he'd dozed off on the chair, that she felt sort of glad Zac hadn't come back with her after all.

Beyond that, she felt very sad indeed.

Chapter Seventeen

The next day saw Zac standing at the bottom of the Tor, second-guessing himself yet again. He'd put a white shirt on and had left his waxed jacket open so people could see he'd at least made an effort to dress appropriately.

Had it been a good idea to come down here, to the other end of the country, and see her? His heart told him yes, yes of course, but his sensible side said he was utterly daft. It was a kind of self-inflicted torture, wasn't it? But he reminded himself of his reasoning – if he saw her, his mind would eventually be settled that she was happy, and he could move on and stop hoping for her to walk across the car park at Skye and call a greeting to him as she opened the tea room door, or smile that beautiful smile at him as she carried a bundle of her prints and a selection of Celtic jewellery into the shop …

But that way madness lay. Zac had always been a dreamer. Was it so wrong that Ivy featured more and more in his dreams? Deep down, he wondered if it was time to get over Ivy and move on with his life, as she had moved on with hers. He should maybe try some of the mindfulness that everyone seemed to embrace down here – that "in the moment" stuff, which would stop him weaving dreams around a life with Ivy McFarlane.

Yes. It probably was time to do that, because he had no real right to expect her to come back to Skye.

But it was so hard. Especially when she had been so close to him last night …

It had, more than likely, been a huge mistake to come here.

He sighed and tried to concentrate on what he was seeing now with his eyes and not dreaming about with his heart. He might as well try to enjoy the experience.

So, what did we have in this consciously mindful moment? Crowds of excited people wandering past him, smiling and chatting, the majority of them dressed in white ... A group of carollers singing songs, dressed, contrastingly, in brightly coloured outfits ... The evocative sounds of the old music wrapping itself around him like gentle strands of greenery; just like holly and ... ivy.

Aye. It was maybe the wrong time of year to be yearning after a lass called Ivy, he thought ironically. He cast a glance at the throng of celebrants and then he saw her. All second guesses fled from his mind as he took some steps towards her, a smile automatically breaking out across his face.

'Ivy!' He waved at her.

She looked around at his voice, her eyes fixed on his, and she waved back, then started hurrying over to him. 'Zac. You came! I'm so pleased.'

'Why wouldn't I? Why would I not come?' He was surprised. No matter what had happened with that kiss – or that non-kiss, because he wasn't going to allow himself to think about it, or to think about the warm taste of mulled wine on her lips – he wasn't going to let her down. 'I said I'd be here, didn't I?'

'Yes, but. After. Well. Aye.' She cleared her throat, the gentle Scottish accent coming to the fore again.

'After last night?' He smiled. 'Aye. I've been thinking about that. And I think the explanation is that I definitely blame the alcohol.'

'Really?'

'Okay. Maybe not entirely. But I think it's best if we both forget it.' He frowned. 'It's probably best that I leave straight after our ceremony things today as well. Before things get even more complicated. I'll leave you to your life down here and slope back off to Skye. I'm glad I came. It's settled my mind a bit, I think. In some ways, anyway.'

'Zac, I—'

'Ivy! Ivy, I'm so pleased you could come today!' A girl with long, reddish hair tied up in dreadlocks with a white ribbon appeared beside them and hugged Ivy. 'I know you were totally excited about it. Hi.' She turned to Zac and smiled, the piercing in her nose reminding him of Angel; the piercing in her bottom lip not so much, as Angel hadn't quite gone there yet. The whole look suited the redhead. 'I'm Zara. I work with Ivy.'

He thought her tongue might also be pierced, as he was sure he'd seen a flash of stainless steel as she spoke.

'Zara's our mindfulness coach. You remember seeing her area in our building?' Ivy offered by way of explanation. There was something in her eyes that implied Zara had come at an entirely inopportune moment, but Ivy was so lovely that she would never make anyone feel unwelcome. She smiled at Zara and her eyes cleared, and whatever had been in that moment drifted off into the snowy mists.

'Oh! Aye. Nice to meet you.' Zac held his hand out to shake Zara's but was taken by surprise as he received an enthusiastic hug instead. Zara laughed at his expression. 'I'm Pagan. You get hugs. You don't get handshakes from me.'

'Hugs are good.' Zac grinned. 'I'm afraid this is all pretty new to me.'

'Are you staying in Glastonbury for a while?' Zara asked, falling into step with them as they began the winding climb up the Tor, the carollers still singing and playing instruments joyously as everyone snaked up the huge hill.

'No. I'm heading home after this. It's a long drive.'

'But you are coming to the Chalice Well, aren't you?' Zara looked concerned. 'You simply have to. We'll be taking the Sacred Flame down there and meditating. Come on.' She nudged him. 'You can't pass up the chance of a water blessing. It's totally magical.'

'Oh! No. Of course. I'll be coming down. That was in our plan, wasn't it?' He looked at Ivy, whose chin was by now tucked into her white scarf, a white bobble hat on her head.

'Yes.' Ivy nodded. 'I said we should do that.' There was a note of defeat in her voice, as if she was hoping to have a more private conversation, but Zara was not to be deflected.

'Awesome.' Zara nodded and they ploughed upwards. 'Isn't Gid coming?'

'No. No, he's busy.'

'Maybe next year then.'

'Maybe,' said Ivy with a shrug. 'I'm not so sure he's that keen on the cold, so who knows what'll happen.' She dipped her head further and Zac got the impression that there was something Ivy didn't really want to share with Zara.

And as for himself, Zac didn't like to think of Ivy still being here next year, and of her doing the Solstice activities with someone else. There was a sense, to him at least, that this was such a special, spiritual thing to do that he couldn't imagine himself wanting to do it with anyone else ever. But that was because he didn't live here and didn't have a partner here and didn't have a life down here – which Ivy clearly did.

Well, she was happy and successful, and that was the most important thing. She'd followed her dreams and it had worked. He'd followed his in a fit of stupidity and a wild hope that he might find her missing him as much as he was missing her.

It was time to concentrate on the Winter Solstice, not dream about things he couldn't change.

And this Tor was something else.

Zac was fit but even he found the climb knocked the wind out of him. It was bloody cold but, oddly, he was enjoying it. He was no stranger to chilly weather, but the snow had dusted the Tor path and it was icy in patches. At one point, he grabbed Ivy's arm as she slipped. He found, despite his new resolve, he didn't really want to let her go; so, he didn't. His excuse, should she ask, would be that he was keeping her safe.

She didn't ask.

Ivy was pleased she didn't have to let go of Zac's hand. It might have been awkward, and she might have said anything in an unguarded moment – but then Zara had appeared with her enthusiastic hugs and excited chatter and that moment was lost.

Which was probably a good thing, because the last thing she wanted to do was crumble in front of Zac. It was magical down here, it really was, especially today – and she wanted to enjoy it and cherish every moment – because who else would be top of her list to do all this with, except Zac?

And now there was a perfectly good excuse to keep holding his hand, as everyone was standing in a big circle around the Tor, and the Sacred Flame was being lit, and someone was calling for blessings from all four directions; the ritual was in full swing.

Ivy didn't know a whole lot about the rituals they were doing, but she knew that it felt absolutely magical, and she didn't want to be anywhere else except on the top of that hill, overshadowed by the tower, holding hands with Zac as the snow flurried around her, and far below them the town bustled with life and love and Christmas blessings of all sorts.

Ivy cast a glance up at Zac as the leader of the celebration sent a message of "love out to the Universe", and he looked as confused as she felt – but confused in a nice way, as he was smiling and mumbling responses to whatever they had to respond to.

And then that was it. The Solstice point came and went, the Solstice blessings rolled on and the circle opened up to whoever needed it. Then it closed down, and they began the winding descent heralded by the Sacred Flame on their way to the Chalice Well.

And she still held his hand.

Zac felt surprisingly at home there, despite the fact that if he thought about it too hard, he realised he'd probably never do this again. He definitely felt welcomed into the Solstice celebrations, though. He made sure he held Ivy's hand tightly as they walked down the Tor, surrounded by groups of like-minded souls. Zara chattered happily and paused halfway to look up to the tower.

'Isn't it beautiful?' she said. 'Oh! I thought that was Morgana there. Hold on. No, no my mistake. If it was her, then—' she turned back to them and held her hands out '—she's gone. Disappeared like smoke into the crowds.'

She grinned. 'Come on. The Chalice Well is really very special.'

And it was. They gathered with the rest of the people, clutching hot drinks and being part of the Wheel of the Year meditation at midday around the well head. Zac closed his eyes and tried to channel the good feelings he had here. He was most conscious, however, of Ivy standing closely beside him, the warmth of her bobble hat tickling his chin, and the fact his hand seemed to find hers yet again. She didn't resist. It was going to be so difficult to leave her.

'Can you wait until two o'clock?' Her whispered voice broke into his thoughts as they stood looking at the intricate metalwork of the well head, the rush of gentle water strangely musical. 'There's another ceremony then. It's around a fire on the Lower Lawn. I understand if you can't, though. It's a long way back. Unless ...' She turned away, her cheeks pink, biting her lip. He knew, without a doubt, what she was going to suggest. Another night at the bed and breakfast. Another night with her.

And it wouldn't end there. Not tonight, not this magical day. No. They'd spend the day together, and it wouldn't end with a kiss under the Christmas tree. Tonight, he knew he would be wanting to love her, heart and soul ... and that just wasn't fair. She wasn't his to love, and it seemed that she felt as powerless to resist the draw to one another as he was.

'I can't.' His voice was soft. He consciously brought an image of Gideon into his mind. Dammit, Gid had been quite a cool person. In another life, in another way, they might even have been friends. But Ivy was Gideon's, and he couldn't do anything to jeopardise that. She had a life here. A life that didn't include him. He shook his head, his voice firmer now, slightly louder. 'I can't. I'm sorry.'

'That's fine.' She seemed to shrink away from him, a small figure bundled into a coat that suddenly looked too big for her. 'I understand. It's a long way back. I'm pleased you managed to stay as long as you did.'

'Me too. It was magical.' He turned towards her. They were still holding hands, he realised, almost with a shock. It had felt as if she belonged there, as if she was part of him, and the feeling wasn't going away anytime soon. He took her other hand in his and pulled her closer. 'I wouldn't have changed today for the world. Or last night. Thank you. Come on. Come with me. I think it looks as if it's a bit more secluded down there. I don't want to have to share you with anyone else just now.'

He released one of her hands and began to lead her down a little pathway that meandered towards a low rectangular pool, hidden away in a small paved courtyard. He was right – there was nobody else around, and he pulled her closer again, took both her hands in his, leaned his forehead against hers and closed his eyes.

'Ivy. If I could stay, I would. If I thought it would change anything, I'd never leave. But I can't. I have to go back.' He leaned down and kissed her, lingering over her lips as if it was the last time he would do this. And it was. In his heart, he knew it was. He couldn't allow it to happen again. That wasn't fair on anyone. 'You would have made me very happy, Ivy, had things been different. As it is, I have to go back, and I have to leave you here. And I can't stay. I'm sorry, but it's not fair on anyone.'

He let her go, ran his thumb down the side of her cheek

and looked at her sadly. He would remember today, he knew he would. But, like all magic, back in the real world it would be different and it would vanish, almost without a trace. She had Gideon, she had a life down here, and who was he to disrupt it?

'I understand, Zac. I do. I don't like how I feel, or how saying goodbye to you today feels, but I understand.' Her voice caught on a sob. 'It doesn't mean that I have to like it, though.'

'Me neither. Look. I'm going now. No. Please, Ivy.' He pressed his fingertips against her lips as she looked as if she was going to protest again. 'I'm parked along the road. I checked out of the bed and breakfast first thing. If I'm going to be honest, after last night, I knew this would happen and I knew if I didn't make a proper effort to leave you, I wouldn't go. Enjoy the rest of the Solstice, and, well … Merry Christmas.' He tried to smile, stole a last lingering look at her, drowned a little in her sea-green eyes, and started to turn away.

'It doesn't make it any easier, does it? I sometimes wish I'd never come here …' It was almost as if she was going to say more. Her lips parted, she blushed, then she caught her lips between her teeth and dropped her head.

'No. No, you can't say that. Look at what you've achieved. You had to do it, and I'm *pleased* you're doing it. Even though it's never been easy saying goodbye to you.' He put his head down and walked as fast as he dared out of the gardens. 'Because I love you, and I don't want to hold you back,' he whispered. 'Which is exactly why I have to go.'

Chapter Eighteen

'Did you have a really *fun* ceremony?'

The question was as loaded as it was delivered in a sickly-sweet Pennsylvanian accent.

Ivy felt a ripple of annoyance that overlaid the barely suppressed tears she was fighting back. She wished Morgana would just get out of her life. She had really had enough today.

'Yes. Thanks.' She busied herself doing some more unnecessary straightening up of her goods and surreptitiously brushed some more dust off a brooch case, her cheeks heating up as she remembered the way she and Zac had parted. Was that really only an hour or so ago?

'Yeah. You looked like you were having some real good fun with that guy who came in the other day. Zac? Yeah?'

Ivy clutched a pendant so tightly she was sure she'd have a Celtic cross marked on her palm forever. Oh well, if that was the case, she could just hold her palm out and Morgana might disintegrate into ashes.

'Aye. Zac.'

'I saw you up on the Tor. Holding hands.'

'Everyone was holding hands.'

'Not to that extent.'

'Whatever.'

'Does Gid know you've been seeing him?'

'Why should that matter?' Ivy couldn't believe she was even being drawn into this conversation. It was none of her business anyway, and no way would she be prepared to sob in front of this woman and say how awful it was that Zac had gone home, and no doubt poor Gid would be getting the brunt of it tonight.

'No reason. Just wondering.'

'Well, it's none of your business, to be honest.'

'Okay.' After a moment, Morgana spoke again. 'I was out last night as well. I saw you under the Christmas tree. Looked intense.' She slithered out of her seat and popped the *Closed* sign on her counter. She gathered up some parcels. 'Anyway. I need to post these. Last minute orders. I told the guys they'd not get there in time for Christmas, but hey, they all insisted. When you have a cool customer base, you gotta maintain it. I'd hate to let my customers down. I'd hate to let anyone down. You gotta manage expectations. It's not nice if you don't.'

'Well, to be fair, I think I was having a much better time last night than you. I did see you, by the way – when I was getting into the taxi. One of us didn't look as if they were having much fun last night, and it certainly wasn't *me*.'

She stopped herself from saying anything else, in case those dams broke and the bitterness and annoyance all ended up directed at Morgana. And Ivy at least knew how Gid would react to the brunt of her temper – he'd probably just laugh at her.

Morgana flushed, then paused for a second as if she was going to say something else; then her face closed up and she almost ran out of the building. Ivy shook her head. She wasn't proud of herself, and she could definitely have said more, but there was only so much a girl could bloody take. And if Morgana was constantly mean to her, well, it was perhaps good that she got a taste of her own medicine.

And on the positive side, if the Wicked Witch of the West was on her travels around Glastonbury, maybe Ivy would get a customer or two, which would hopefully take her mind off Zac.

But, even as she inwardly grumbled about Morgana, she was aware that the warm, fuzzy, mulled-wine feeling Zac had instilled in her that morning hadn't quite evaporated. Part of her could still feel his arms around her; an embrace that seemed to mean more than just a "Merry Christmas" between friends. It had been an embrace that seemed to be all at once a declaration of some deeper, hidden feelings and almost a goodbye, as if he was releasing her from his life with those few whispered words: '*You would have made me very happy, Ivy, had things been different.*' Had what been different, though? Him and her? Their attitude to one another? The way their lives had diversified?

She pressed her lips together, remembering the feeling of his mouth against hers and blinked back a silly tear or two. She was no further forward. Having him down here had made the last two days so wonderful. It had reconnected her with herself, almost; just like the time on Skye when they had climbed his beloved mountains, the time they'd no doubt both remembered as they stood at the bottom of the Tor that Solstice morning ...

So yes. The whole fabulous energy vibe that practically twinkled around Glastonbury, and the peaceful meditation and ceremony at the Chalice Well which had grounded her so nicely, were still in her heart, but she knew Zac had taken a huge chunk of it back to Skye with him.

And here she was, facing Christmas. It was her self-appointed decision time and, ironically, the way Zac had turned up out of the blue then walked away from her had made that decision even harder. He had been so positive, and when he was talking to her, she almost believed that she was the success she pretended she was. Ivy wasn't a girl who gave up on her dreams too quickly, but she also had to be realistic.

The bell on the door jingled and she looked up, hoping with all of her heart that it was him again – that he'd driven only so far up the M5 motorway, then turned around and come back for her.

'Ives!' No such luck. It was Gid, followed closely by Tallulah. Tallulah was clutching a steaming takeaway hot chocolate with whipped cream dripping down the sides, and Gid was looking pained.

'I need you, Ives,' Gid continued, blinking huge puppy-dog eyes at her, as Tallulah squeezed past him, holding her cup well out of harm's way. 'Desperately.'

Ivy was used to Gid's dramatic declarations, but they didn't usually come when he was sober.

'Is it an emergency?'

'Totes. Yeah. I need you to come and have a look at something. Or someone.'

'Someone? As in?'

'Zara. She wants a tatt. She's been inspired by the ceremony today, and it's her Yuletide gift to herself. But she doesn't just want any tatt. She wants a copy of your lino print thing.' He waved his hand at the arrangement of cards behind Ivy. 'The Tor one. The one with the stars and things on.'

'Oh! That one. My van Gogh inspired one?' Ivy grinned, despite herself. 'It's my favourite.' She had taken her lead from that great artist and superimposed the Tor on a background of something quite similar to his *Starry Night* picture.

'I'm scared, Ives. Really scared.' Gid pulled a face, comical in its forlornness. 'What if I mess it up? Then I'll kind of lose two friends. You'll hate me for ruining your vision, and she'll hate me for ruining *her.*'

Ivy laughed. 'So, what do you need me for?'

'Supervision.' Gid nodded, seriously. 'So you can tell me if the way I've marked it out looks okay.'

'You're certainly getting some interesting pictures to do at the minute. I hope the dragon man was okay in the end! All right, come on. I'll supervise you.'

'Thanks, Ives. I'll buy you an extra Christmas present.' Perhaps there was a little more Christmas spirit lurking in Gid than she had thought.

'An extra one? So, you're deciding to celebrate then?'

'Maybe. Here's a proposition for you: I may run to a lit-up twig.'

Ivy rolled her eyes in an exaggerated fashion, then grabbed her coat. She came out from behind the counter and Gid grinned, slinging his arm around her, guiding her out. This would be interesting.

'Tallulah, can you watch the counter for me?' she called.

Tallulah raised her hot chocolate and smiled back. 'Sure. I'll watch Morgana's too – doubt there'll be anyone here, but I've got an appointment in five minutes. I can probably stave her off until one of you is back, though.'

'Thanks, Tal.' Ivy smiled, then headed out with Gid. 'So, my friend, can I charge you a copyright fee?'

'You can try. But then I can't afford your twig.'

They were laughing, and half-way along the path, when Morgana passed them on the way back from the post office.

'Oh! Hey.' Gid stopped and grinned, pulling Ivy closer

to him. 'I'm just stealing Ives away for a bit. It's a highly secret mission involving the Tor, a proposition and the fact I need her desperately.' He dropped a kiss on Ivy's head affectionately and laughed. 'I'll have her back soon. Sorry, there's only Tallulah there at the minute and she said she'd keep an eye out for customers for you guys, but I think you're pretty safe. She's got someone coming in, though.'

Morgana stared at them, and Ivy could have sworn she paled beneath the already pale make-up. 'Oh ... sure,' Morgana stammered out. Then she nodded, pulled her cloak around her and hurried away, disappearing into the shop like a phantom of the night.

But Ivy had no more thoughts to waste on Morgana – she'd irritated her quite enormously already this morning. She needed to reclaim her good vibes. On a positive note, this tattoo was going to be incredibly interesting and Gid was dragging her along quite quickly.

It was pretty cold and the fresh air stung her cheeks. She was pleased she'd had the foresight to put her coat on. In contrast, Gid had wandered out into the snowy streets with nothing more than a T-shirt and a pair of cargo shorts on. Typical Gid.

Zac had lost the plot. He had completely lost the plot.

It was going to take him until next year to get home at this rate. He'd already managed to add another couple of hours onto his journey by pulling this little trick.

He swung his Range Rover into a space at the Abbey, thanking his lucky stars for such a convenient place to throw his car into when he was on a mission, before launching himself out of the door, running as fast as he could to Celtic

163

Heart, ready to try again. Slip-roads that led to roundabouts on the motorway were very convenient things.

'Ivy!' He threw the door open, looking around, seeing the place was more or less empty apart from Morgana.

Morgana looked up, startled, as he burst through the door and, in the absence of anyone else, Zac took a couple of long strides and stood in front of her. 'Morgana. Is Ivy around?'

'Ivy?' She stared at him through red-rimmed eyes for a moment. She looked as if she had been crying. A strange expression flickered across her face but, in an instant, it was gone. She cleared her throat and looked at him, straight in the eye. 'No. Gid took her off somewhere. I bumped into them in the street. He said he had a proposition for her. And that he needed her. So.' She shrugged her shoulders. 'Your guess is as good as mine.'

'A proposition?' The word made him go hot and cold all over. The little shop swam in front of his eyes for a second, until he blinked the wavy lines away. 'Right. Do you know where they went?'

'Gid mentioned the Tor. Beyond that, I have no clue.' Her eyes were suddenly flinty and shuttered, her voice cold. 'You know. I've told people before now it's not a great idea to mess with people's relationships. I may be many things, but some things are kind of sacred. You shouldn't walk all over a relationship. I'd never do it myself, even though I dream about doing it.' She dropped her head and pushed some bits of jewellery around the counter-top. 'So, I think it would be kinda cool if you just go and don't come back. There's no point.'

Zac was thrown. What on earth did she mean? It seemed

that this was a not-so-gentle warning off. But what was all of this about a proposition – and Gid *needing* Ivy?

He swallowed, cringing inwardly. 'Right. So, you're saying Gid and Ivy are together and it's truly pointless me being here. Okay. Well. Thanks for that. I wasn't sure.' He knew if he admitted this to Angel that she would take the moral high ground as well. Perhaps Morgana and Angel were a little more alike than he thought. 'It will definitely be kinda cool if I leave them to it.' The words, originally spoken in an American drawl, sounded odd coming from him. But the sentiment was the same. 'I have no idea what I was thinking.' He raked his hand through his hair and shook his head. 'I need to let this go. I do. Thanks. Thanks very much. Don't … don't tell her I was here.' He nodded again, not waiting for an answer, and turned out of the shop. Back the way he came.

It was, as Morgana said, pointless. A proposition, on Glastonbury Tor, on the Winter Solstice, so close to Christmas. What could be more perfect for Ivy McFarlane?

Nothing. He had no right to come back here after they'd said goodbye. He had too much respect for Ivy, and this was his problem now. He just wanted her to be happy, and it seemed that she was. It seemed that all her Christmas dreams and wishes might have come true for her – but his hadn't. No way.

But what could he do? It was her life and her happiness, and he needed to stay out of it.

The road seemed twice as long going back. But this time, he knew he wouldn't be returning.

Chapter Nineteen

'Honestly, it looks stunning.' Ivy was sitting next to Zara as her friend lay on her tummy, clutching the edge of the table and screwing her face up in trepidation.

'This seemed such a good idea at the time!' Zara winced as Gid seemed to rev the needle up, then grinned at Ivy over Zara's back.

'It *is* a good idea. Honestly, I can use you for free advertising in the summer. Sit naked from the waist up with your back to the door, and I'll make sure everyone knows it was my picture that inspired your tattoo.' Ivy laughed.

'I actually think a nice quote would have been simpler,' said Zara, gasping as Gid set to work. 'Less pain. Ouch!'

Ivy reached over and took Zara's hand. It looked as if she wasn't going to be heading back to Celtic Heart any time soon. But what did it matter? Supporting Zara was more important, and she probably wouldn't have any customers anyway.

'And not naked!' Zara continued, indignantly, through gritted teeth. 'Halter-neck top. Would work. Ouch! *Gid*!'

'Sorry, love.' Gid grinned again, thoroughly enjoying himself it seemed. 'Shall I put a robin or something on it? Something festive? Just about here?'

He pressed his fingertip gently on Zara's shoulder blade, well away from any design, and she sucked her breath in. 'I thought you were sticking the *needle* in me! Not your bloody finger!'

'Gid!' Ivy raised her eyebrows. 'Stop being mean. It's Christmas.'

'Solstice!' muttered Zara. 'And no, you're not drawing any gods on me either.'

Unbelievably, after her encounter with Morgana, Ivy realised she was enjoying herself – and it was taking her mind off Zac, which was the important thing.

After a good hour or so, Ivy was finally released back to Celtic Heart. She was still amused at Gid and Zara as she pushed the door open. Surprisingly, Tallulah was the only person there.

'Thank you for looking after the counter,' Ivy said. 'Did anyone come in?'

'One or two people. Morgana said someone had come in when I had my client, but she said they didn't stay. Then she said a couple of people had come in looking for Zara but said they'd come back tomorrow and see her at the pub later, so I think they were just friends of hers. I can't believe how quiet it's been here today.'

'I can.' Ivy's voice was wry. She was never rushed off her feet, not really. 'Maybe it's because we're tucked away a bit and everyone has been concentrating on the Tor and the Wells with it being Solstice? Some of the guys I talked to at Chalice Well said they were heading to the White Spring. I wouldn't be surprised if that's where the majority of the people are today.'

Ivy had been brave enough to step into the Temple Pool at the White Spring in the summer. One day, sometime in the future, she intended to go deeper into the Healing Pool – but Gid had told her the White Spring held Faerie Portals and was a gateway to the Celtic Otherworld, and the little thrills she had felt hearing that, delicious as they were, had scared her a teeny tiny bit, so she wasn't *quite* brave enough to submerge herself just yet.

Plus, the memory of the sacred spring at Ashaig beach had popped into her mind quite unexpectedly as soon as she'd dipped her toe into the water ...

'Maybe.' Tallulah nodded her agreement. 'I'm sure we'll make up for it tomorrow. I'm heading off now anyway. You?'

'No. I'm going to stay a bit longer. Gid won't be finished for a while, and he's going to come and collect me. We're going to have a takeaway for dinner, and I might as well take the opportunity to do some work when ...' She stopped herself from expanding on that, because much as she liked Tallulah, she didn't want to get into Morgana's attitude problems.

'That's okay.' Tallulah grinned. 'I know what you mean. But she's in love with him, you know? That's why she's the way she is.'

'What?' Ivy blinked at her. 'Who are you talking about?'

'Morgana. She's secretly in love with your Gideon. Has been for months, maybe even longer. Then you came along and she's had her nose pushed right out of joint. She doesn't realise that a woman of my talents can see right into someone's heart. It's easy when you know how.'

'Hold on – *my* Gideon? He's not *my* Gideon. He's just a friend!' And crumbs, hadn't she joked about that very scenario with Zac on the way to the café that first day? When she'd said she went home to him and Morgana went home to a raven and an open coffin? It was a throwaway comment – there was no way she'd actually *believed* it.

'You *say* that, but let's face it, you live together. What's a girl to think? Personally, *I* think she thought she had a chance before you moved in with him. Anyway.' Tallulah stood up. 'None of my business, hard as it might be for me to stay out of things that are blatantly bloody obvious. Okay, I'll see you in the morning. Enjoy the rest of the day. I'm going to bring mince pies and mulled wine in tomorrow. I think we'll be busier, and food and alcohol are good ways to tempt customers into staying a bit longer – in my experience, anyway. See you then.'

Tallulah waved her farewells and vanished into the darkening evening, leaving Ivy staring after her, light finally – and ironically, perhaps – dawning on the Winter Solstice. It made sense then. It all made sense. Morgana's veiled little comments and her apparently unreasonable dislike of her. Especially when – oh goodness! – she had seen Zac and Ivy cosying up on the Tor. And kissing under the Christmas tree.

She must look like a terrible person! And she had to put Morgana right just as soon as she could.

And hadn't Zac called him "your Gideon" as well ... oh *God*! It was suddenly much worse than she'd thought – and she didn't need to be a tarot reader to see where that one might be heading ...

It was late when Zac reached the west of Scotland. It was horribly late, and he was shattered. He pulled into a lay-by and laid his head back against the headrest. Two hours or so to go and he had the joy of an empty croft to look forward to, even though it was a stunning renovation of an old croft. It would still be cold and lonely and, for once, he didn't really want to be on his own there. He hadn't even put a bloody tree up, had he? Beyond that thing on the old ruin. And, much as he wanted to decompress and breathe the island air, he was more in need of sleep and a hot drink and some human company that he could just relax into.

He looked at his phone, saw how close to midnight it was, and shook his head. It was still worth a try, so he dialled his best friend's mobile.

'Angel? I'm sorry to call so late. And I'm not at home, before you ask. I have good reason to be calling you at this daft time of night.'

'Zachary Fallon, my dark horse of a friend. Wherefore art thou tonight, then?'

'Don't let Jessie hear you say that,' he replied wearily, referring to Angel's bookish sister. '"Wherefore" in a Shakespearean sense means "why". Like in *Romeo and Juliet*. "Wherefore art thou Romeo?" – she's asking why he's called Romeo. Why the *hell* am I explaining that to you?'

'I don't know, Zac. I prefer my version. But okay. *Where* art thou tonight then?'

Zac stared at the night-time vista. The odd vehicle passed him, sleet falling in spikes across the headlamps, and he shivered. 'In the middle of bloody nowhere. On a road. In the Highlands. And I calculate I'm closer to Taigh Fallon than I am to my home.'

There was a shriek from the other end of the phone. 'Then you have to come here. We are not allowing you to drive past. What the hell is the idea anyway? Shouldn't you be in Glastonbury? Or – *oh* – is Ivy there with you? We have plenty of room for you both. Come right now!'

'No. No, she's not with me. And you know what. I wish she was here. But that's my problem. Not yours.'

'Oh, Zac. Come here. Immediately. Tell me all about it. I'll have a hot drink ready for you and Kyle can find some whisky. We can put the world to rights.'

'I'd like that.' Zac smiled into the phone. He was grateful

he had Angel in his life – more grateful at this moment than he could really tell her.

And as much as he protested about being on the mainland, a diversion to Taigh Fallon was preferable to two more hours alone with his thoughts on a snowy night.

He was, of course, welcomed with open arms – quite literally as Angel threw herself at him, tumbling out of the front door at him before he'd even reached it.

'Zac. Come in. What's happened?' She rubbed his back as if he was a child. 'I can tell there's something wrong, I can just *tell*.'

'It's pretty obvious that's the case. Why else would he be lurking about on the mainland?' Kyle stepped forward and gave him a quick hug.

'Why else indeed.' Zac dropped his case thankfully onto the hallway floor and saw the big Christmas tree they had told him about, all lit up and cheerful, and smelling deliciously of pine. 'Nice tree.'

'The one you're more familiar with is through here – like we said.' Angel took his hand and dragged him into the lounge, where she sat him quite firmly on a sofa. He felt the tension leaving his shoulders and saw, out of the corner of his eyes, the Goth fairy on the top of the fluffy black tree. 'I bet you haven't got yours up, have you?'

'Have I heck. Hello, gorgeous.' He forced a smile in the direction of the fairy. 'She still looks like you.'

'Of course. She has good taste.' Angel grinned. She was wrapped in her black satin robe, her face pale and scrubbed of make-up, her hair hanging in two long plaits and looking so dearly familiar that Zac knew he was in danger of spilling the whole story out. His own face must have shown it, as he felt Kyle's touch firmly on his shoulder and a glass of whisky was pressed into his hand.

And that was the catalyst. He did indeed spill the whole sorry tale out – even the lies about the Bristol diversion and the random cousins that Angel had, obviously, never heard of.

And even the faint hint of Christmases past and lives long gone that lingered gently on at Taigh Fallon – as the place, according to the fanciful Angel, was haunted by its previous residents – seemed to retreat into the shadows and let him tell his best friend and his cousin about what an absolute eejit he was.

At breakfast-time Zac wandered into the kitchen and saw that Angel was already there.

'Good morning.' She looked up from buttering her toast and smiled. 'Kyle's just down by the Loch. He decided to do a run around it before breakfast.' She shuddered. 'Madness. Pure madness. I bet he doesn't make it all the way around. And it's snowed overnight. Very festive.' She applied a liberal coating of jam, then popped the slice of toast in her mouth, bit off a corner and chewed thoughtfully. 'But I've been thinking, Zac. About Ivy. Do you reckon Gid really proposed to her? Like properly proposed?'

Zac shrugged, helping himself to coffee from the percolator. There were a lot more mod-cons in Taigh Fallon since the springtime, when they'd lined the counter with jars of instant coffee and tubs of chocolate spread to put on their toast. Kyle had done a bit of sympathetic improvement work there, and Angel looked particularly at home – especially, he noted, with her black fluffy mules on her feet. She hadn't bothered dressing yet and was still in her red satin night dress.

'I don't know. I haven't dared check my phone. I don't really want to know.' He smiled thinly. 'It seemed like Morgana expected that to have happened.'

'Morgana.' Angel's lip curled like a dismissive Elvis impersonator. '*That's* not a real name.'

'Now, now.' Zac pushed her shoulder gently. 'You never know.'

'She's just living up to an image.' Angel bit off another piece of toast, quite brutally, Zac thought.

'You don't have the monopoly on Victoriana. Or Goth.'

'I know. But she sounds awful.'

'She looked as annoyed as I felt. And actually a bit upset.'

'Just annoyed and upset that someone else was getting attention.'

'You don't even know her!'

'I don't care. She's upset *you*!' Angel pressed her lips firmly together, and Zac dipped his head and allowed himself a small smile. It was good to be bantering with his friend again. Kyle had, he remembered, also been on the wrong side of Angel's morals when she had first met him – Zac could laugh now at her reaction when he told her how his cousin used to tease him when they were smaller. Oh, how Angel had made Kyle suffer for that one …

'Anyway!' The sudden, harsh, loud tone of Angel's voice made him jump and slop some coffee onto the table-top. 'You need to be an Edgar and woo her.'

'Angel! What on earth are you talking about? Not *Wuthering Heights* again?'

'Damn right, it's *Wuthering Heights*.' Angel nodded, as if she had just made everything in the world all right. 'You're an Edgar. More than that, you're *my* Edgar.' She leaned over and kissed his cheek. 'Me and you, we'd never have worked. I need someone like Kyle. He's my Heathcliff. Edgar was too nice for me. *You* are too nice for me.' Zac found himself nodding in agreement. It was a conversation they'd had before. 'But Edgar was a decent bloke under all the wishy-washyness. Apart from kicking his sister out when she had an affair with Heathcliff though, I guess—'

'You're saying I'm wishy-washy? Ange, you always tell everyone Edgar is pathetic!' Zac didn't know whether to laugh or be insulted. 'And I wouldn't kick my sister out of anywhere. Even if I had one.'

'No! No, you're not wishy-washy and neither are you pathetic. You have hidden depths. And if you had a sister, she wouldn't be like Isabella Linton, not at all. She would be *nice*.' She patted him gently on the hand. Her fingers were sticky with butter and jam, and Zac surreptitiously wiped his hand on his jeans. 'You just need to channel that Edgar-ness into your own nice girl. A nice girl like Ivy. You'd never be the passionate sort. Or the spontaneous sort. Hey. Would you kick one of *my* sisters out?' The question was as random as it was abrupt.

'What? *No!* No, I wouldn't kick Rosa or Jessie out of anywhere! And I beg to differ.' Zac *was* a little insulted now. 'I drove to sodding Glastonbury to find her.' He paused for a second. 'Twice. Aye. Technically, I did it twice.' He brandished two fingers at Angel to prove his point.

'And you came back without her.' Angel sighed. 'Oh Zac. Right – after Christmas, you're going back down.'

'No! No, I'm not. I said my goodbyes to her. She's with Gideon. She's happy.' He pushed his coffee cup away angrily and sat back in the seat. 'She's living with him. He proposed to her on the Tor. On the Solstice! She's got a lovely little business down there. She's not coming back, Ange. She's never going to come up here for Christmas with me, ever.'

But, to his surprise, Angel shrieked with laughter and clapped her hands. 'That, my love, is the passion you need to show her.' Then she shook her head and sighed. 'Oh, Zac. Honestly. Realistically, you're not going to achieve anything before Christmas, so we need to think about it. For a start, we don't even know if he did propose. She certainly hasn't messaged me, and I would have thought she would have done. Especially if she couldn't get in touch with you.'

'I'm sure we'll find out. Okay. I can't take advantage of Judith any longer, so when Kyle comes back, I must get ready to go. I can be back for lunchtime and just … pick up where I left off. I guess.'

'No, you can't.' Angel had that smug tone to her voice that could, on occasion, irritate Zac if it was directed at him. 'Because now you've had, what, twenty-four hours in Ivy's company? And a lot can change in twenty-four hours.'

'Twenty-one hours. Give or take.'

'Not that you're counting.' Angel smiled sympathetically, and patted him with those jammy fingers again. 'It'll work out. Listen to a genuine Christmas Angel.' She pointed to herself and grinned. 'Seriously, though, I'd work some magic if I could for you. But, I'm afraid it's between you and Ivy now, and we can't do anything until we know exactly what happened with Gideon yesterday.'

Zac didn't think he really wanted to know.

Chapter Twenty

Morgana wasn't in the shop the next morning, which Ivy felt a little bad about. She desperately needed to speak to her about Gideon. Zara, however, was there and was wincing with every movement – and yes, crackling slightly as her clothing rubbed against the cling-film covering her new body art. But she was cheerful and told everyone who would listen about the tattoo and where she had got the design from, and it lifted Ivy's spirits enormously.

Ivy made a conscious effort to push Morgana to the back of her mind and just enjoy the day. The twenty-second of December. Three days until Christmas. Then she would have to make her decision. She knew which way she was tempted to go when she thought of Zac's rather intense dark eyes and his slow, quiet smile ... but still. On a day like today, she was *enjoying* herself here.

Zara, being the good friend she was, had actually bought one of Ivy's prints and not asked for a freebie as some people might. She was displaying the print on her desk, as well as taking it into the quiet room and asking her clients to concentrate on it as part of their mindfulness therapy. As a result, Ivy had quite a fun day and sold quite a few copies of the print as people were so thoroughly enthused with Zara's workshops that they were happy and willing to part with their money. The sale of the prints had a knock-on effect on the rest of her stock, and she enjoyed the most successful day she'd had in a while.

'Christmas is a stressful time,' Zara told Ivy. 'More people should learn to zone out and not overthink things. It's part of my job to make that happen.'

'I'm definitely one for overthinking,' admitted Ivy, in a lull between customers, mid-afternoon. Tallulah had provided them with paper cups of mulled wine and a mince pie each, and the three women were chatting amiably. 'I'm still not sure I made the right decision by coming here. Or by staying here.' She felt her cheeks grow warm as she realised it was the first time she had admitted that to any of her friends down here, apart from Gid. And that was only because she had told him she needed a place to stay.

'We're not so bad!' Zara laughed.

'No! You're both lovely. You and Tal …' She shut up before she said too much.

'But not Morgana.' Tal grinned. 'I told you why. She loves your Gid, that's why.'

'Please – he's *not* my Gid. And it's not my problem. If she wants him, she can have him. I'm not going to stop her. But I don't want her hanging around the flat if they do get together.'

'Why ever not?' Tal refilled her cup.

'Because it's a one-bedroom place and my domain is the sofa. God, I can hear Gid snoring. Imagine if I heard anything else!'

'Awkward!' Zara laughed. '*Very* awkward.'

'And besides that, Morgana hates me. She absolutely detests me—'

'I think you'll find it's more the way you're treating Gideon that I hate.' The voice was cold, proclaiming the details over the *ding* of the bell as Morgana flung the door open.

'Morgana!' Ivy almost choked on her drink. She almost

apologised – but she stopped herself. Why on earth should she apologise for Morgana overhearing what Morgana's opinion on Ivy was? It's not like she was saying *she* hated Morgana. She sat up straighter and stared at the woman in the doorway.

'Oops. *Très* awkward. Tal, fancy a spot of meditation in the quiet room?' Zara asked. 'I think Ivy might need some space. Unless you want us as back-up, Ives?'

Ivy simply shook her head. What she had to say needed saying. It was time to do it, and the mulled wine had at least given her a little bit of Dutch courage.

'Meditation sounds perfect.' Tal picked up her cup and the remains of her pie. 'Give us a shout if you need us,' she added in a whisper to Ivy. 'We'll not be far.'

Again, Ivy nodded, but her attention was focused on Morgana.

Her nemesis looked like she hadn't slept. Her normally perfectly styled hair was frizzy around the ends, and one of the reasons she looked so weird was that she didn't have industrial amounts of eyeliner on today. No, her hair was pulled back in a ponytail, frizzy ends and all, and her make-up was non-existent. Plus, she was wearing jeans and a sweater and Ugg boots.

'Yes. It's me. I'm not staying, don't worry. I can't actually bear to be in the same room as you today, Ivy.'

'Why? What have I *ever* done to you?' Ivy had *definitely* had enough. All her good resolutions about having an adult, supportive talk with Morgana where she gave her blessing for her to be with Gid, if that was what she so desired, fled as her temper boiled over once again. She was really getting her money's worth out of her temper, which was very unlike her.

'I know you like Gid. Well, I know now. But that's no reason to treat me like you do.'

'I didn't tell you how I felt about him, because that's not cool,' continued Morgana. 'But F.Y.I. I've known him a while now, and we were getting close – then he told me all about this girl he knew, this really cool, crazy, arty chick from Scotland and how she was coming down here and how she hoped to start a new life and how he couldn't wait for her to come. Then you were here for six months, and you moved in with him! I've known him for two years and I really thought I was special. Then *you* came. And I couldn't compete.' Her voice caught on a weird little sob and Ivy stared at her, completely thrown. This awful woman was, apparently, as human and vulnerable as the next person. 'My ex went off with an art student one Christmas, and I ran away instead of fighting for him. I came here, and I was in a bad place, and met Gid. He knew, *he knew* what I was like underneath and he made me feel safe and helped me to start again. And I thought ...' Her voice broke and she wiped a tear away angrily. 'I thought I could make a future ... with him in it. Then *you* turned up.'

'I *did* turn up. I had a dream I needed to follow. And now I've tried it and failed, I don't think I should be here any more. Not really.'

Morgana glared at her with a flash of the old bitterness. 'Then you should have told him. You should have broken up with him properly before you went with that Zac guy. Before Gid proposed to you. Nobody should treat anybody like that, and I can't stand aside and watch you do it. Not to him.'

'*Proposed* to me?' Ivy sat down, stunned. 'Never. He's never done that. He wouldn't. We're just friends.'

'Just *friends*? You live together! And what about what

he said yesterday?' Morgana challenged her. 'He had a proposition for you. He needed you, and he was taking you to the Tor. On the Solstice! It was damn perfect. I wish someone would do that for me! I told that guy where you'd gone. I had to tell him. I might not be able to have Gid, but you're damn well not having him *and* someone else.'

'Woah – yesterday?' Ivy was thoroughly confused.

'Yes. When I saw you on the street.' Another tear dripped off Morgana's nose. 'What he said to me.'

'His *proposition* was that he would buy a Christmas tree for the flat if I agreed to have a look at Zara's new tattoo – well, a lit-up Christmas twig. And Zara's tattoo is of the Tor – and based on one of my lino prints. That was why he *needed* me! To make sure I was happy with it. We are *not* together. And can I give you some advice?' She was livid, and she didn't wait for an answer. 'You'd have been more likely to get to first base, or whatever you want to call it, with Gid if you were actually *nice* to me. Because then, you see, I'd have gone home – where F.Y.I. I sleep on his *sofa* because I couldn't afford the rent on another place of my own – and I'd go, "oh Gid, I had a really great day with Morgana today. She's really cool and really lovely and we work together so well". But no. No – you chose to turn against me from the moment we met, and there was no reason to. You never once tried to be friends or to be supportive in any way. You just assumed we were a couple. Well, news flash, we're not and never have been!'

Morgana turned even paler and it was her turn to sit down. 'You're not?'

'No! You never bothered to ask me, or to get to know me or to find out anything about me. Gid and I were friends at art college, and we came to Glastonbury on a college trip years ago. We did our work placements here at the same time. He knew I always wanted to come back and work here – in fact, we both did. He just got here first – and good for him, he's happy and he's made a success of things. That didn't happen for me, and, if I'm being brutally honest, you didn't help. You just sabotaged my whole business and yes, I hope you're happy, because I'm leaving. I am definitely leaving. I'm going back home to Scotland. You've made my decision for me. I don't want to work anywhere with someone who treats me like you do. I deserve better and I'm worth more than that.'

'Oh God. I'm sorry. I'm so *sorry*.' Morgana looked up at her, horror in her eyes as realisation apparently dawned. 'I really am. Please. Don't leave on account of me. I'll sort myself out. I'll stop behaving like a brat …'

'Oh, please. It's not *all* on account of you. I'm a grown up. I suspect we could move on from it. Although I'll be honest, it's been horrible at times.' Ivy sighed and drained her paper cup of mulled wine. 'It's just not the place for me. I'd come back and visit like a shot – but my heart isn't in it. It's not here. I can't explain it.'

'Ivy?' Morgana suddenly sounded contrite, her voice small. 'That guy I mentioned before. The one I said I'd told where you were?'

'Aye?' Ivy's voice was cautious, and despite herself, little bubbles of fear and anxiety began to prickle in her stomach. She knew, she just *knew* what Morgana was going to say …

'It was Zac. He came back yesterday. You were out. With Gid.' She dropped her head. 'I told him to go home and not come back. That you were with Gid, and he shouldn't mess with people's relationships. That it was pointless. I am *so* sorry.'

'He came back? After he'd *left*?'

Morgana nodded. 'Yes.'

'Oh God.' Ivy grabbed her phone. 'I need to tell him what happened. I need to let him know it's fine.'

She fumbled with the phone, dialling his number, texting him. But there was no answer. Nothing. Well, she couldn't stay here now, could she? Not at all.

She ran out of the shop and then all the way home. He'd done it. He'd cut her off, set her free. What else would someone like Zac do? He would think it was for the best. And if she couldn't reach him on the phone ... well. There were other ways to find him again.

Chapter Twenty-One

'Good evening!' Gid swept in to the flat as she was throwing clothes into a case. He was still in those wretched shorts. 'There's some carollers in the square.' He jerked his thumb over his shoulder. 'Under the Christmas tree. Thought you might like to go, then nip to the King Will for a pint or three. Look.' He unfurled his other hand and in his palm was a wooden star. 'I liberated this from the shop. I think this might make a pretty cool decoration for our twig, don't you? Damn! I still need to *get* the twig though, don't I?'

'Gid! Shut up about your twig. It's a lovely thought, but I don't think I'll be here for Christmas. Look! Just look around you!' She waved her hand at the mess in the lounge. 'I'm going. I'm going back up to Skye. I need to get in touch with Zac. I need to …' She started shaking uncontrollably. 'I can't call him. I can't get through.'

'Woah! You're going nowhere today, girl. Nowhere.' He put his hands on her shoulders. 'It's pitch black out there. How long do you think it would take you to get up there? Like, twelve hours or something stupid? You'd be driving through the night, and get there at stupid o'clock in the morning. Stop being so … spontaneous. Yeah?'

Gid was one of the most laidback people Ivy knew, apart from Zac, so it shouldn't have been a surprise to her that his presence managed to calm her down. She took a couple of deep breaths, knowing he was right.

'And anyway, what are you going back there for?' He was curious, not annoyed or disappointed or anything like that.

'Did you finally decide?' He'd known of course that she was wobbling, but had always trusted her to come to her own conclusions. He was a good enough friend not to try and influence her in any way.

Ivy nodded. She didn't trust herself to speak.

'Well then. I'm sorry my sofa couldn't make you stay.' He smiled, then pulled her close in a hug. 'You tried though. You gave it a damn good go. It's not for everyone. What was it that made you decide? Because if it's just stress, you know, from Christmas and the like, I can get Zara to give you some mindfulness tips.'

Despite herself, she smiled. 'No. It's not Christmas stress. I've loved the build-up down here. It was so special up on the Tor at the Solstice, and down at the Wells, but ...' She tailed off.

'But that was partially because you shared those experiences with Zac?'

'Yes.' There was no point denying it. 'Yes. They would still have been special, but he made it more special.'

'Cool. That's a cool reason to go home. You know you've always got a second home here though, don't you?'

'I do. Thank you.'

'Your sofa will always be yours,' he said mock-seriously, and this time she laughed properly.

There was a ring on the doorbell and Gid grumbled something about unsociable hours, then went to the door to open it. Over his shoulder, Ivy saw that Morgana was standing there, looking a lot more composed than she had done when Ivy had left her at Celtic Heart.

'I'm sorry to be a nuisance,' said Morgana, her voice stilted, her cheeks tinged with pink. It was odd to see her with colour in her face. 'But I couldn't leave things as they were. Ummm … I kind of think you'll be heading back to Skye for a while, and I also kind of know you've got a shop full of stock at Celtic Heart. Are you taking it with you? Because it's just a deadweight at the minute. For you, that is,' she added quickly, apparently seeing the sour expression Ivy could feel forming on her face at the word "deadweight". 'You'll not be making any money on any of it. So, I kinda want to make a proposition myself.' Morgana blushed even more. 'I can sell it through my counter, if you want? I'll add it to the online shop, and you'll get one hundred per cent profit off the sales, I promise. It's just, I think it'll go pretty well. And then it's kinda moving forward for you. And if you do want to come back, your space is there, and I'll share it better. Or if you don't, you'll still have a foothold in Glasto, because I'll keep stock in for you. If you want.' She shrugged and dug her hands in her pockets. 'Just a thought. You don't have to trust me, I guess. It could all go in the dumpster tomorrow, as much as you *do* trust me. But you've got a good right to feel like that. I'm not making excuses.'

Ivy stared at her, processing the information. Was Morgana being *nice* to her?

'Look.' Morgana appeared even more uncomfortable and clearly felt as if she needed to expand a bit. 'I've been horrible. I know I have. I'm trying to make up for it. What with it being Christmas and all. The season of goodwill.' She attempted what might have been a small, apologetic smile. She looked younger, more attractive. Ivy wished this girl, this version of Morgana, had been the one she knew from Celtic Heart and not the black-hearted terror she had grown used to over the last few months.

She felt a little contrite herself for the way she'd blown up at Morgana earlier, and her own cheeks grew warm. But it had needed to be said, most definitely. The air needed to be cleared – and hopefully it almost was.

'Christmas. Yes. Okay. I'd be very grateful if you would do that for me, Morgana.' What was the point of keeping such a silly feud going? As Morgana said, it was a time for goodwill.

'Morgana.' The woman half-smiled. 'Sure. It's Megan. Morgana just sounds better for this place. I'm not really *her*.'

Ivy finally smiled, properly. 'Megan. I thought Morgana was a bit of a cover-story.' There was a beat. 'I think I'd like Megan. I'd like to get to know her better.' Ivy moved over to Gideon and squeezed his hand. 'And I can guarantee that Gid will still be around, so once I'm out of his hair, you'll be able to be yourself with him.'

Gideon was looking at Morgana – or Megan – with a new sense of respect. And, Ivy was pleased to note, a certain dopey kind of awe. In fact, he looked like a puppy dog who realised he had found his forever home. It was as if he was seeing her for who she really was, for the very first time. She suspected he'd never really known Megan – only the hideous veneer that was apparently Morgana.

'Cool.' Megan/Morgana gave a smile, and there was untold relief in it. 'I'll disappear now and let you get sorted. You'd better give me your contact details though, then we can chat about it properly. Or email. If you don't want to chat.' She flushed again. 'I understand.'

'Chatting is fine. And thanks.'

'No worries. And … good luck with Zac. He seems like a nice guy.'

'He is.' Ivy's stomach lurched – a little bit of nerves, and a little bit of anticipation, she thought. 'I'll find out soon enough if he's prepared for the Christmas miracle of me arriving on his doorstep. I'll keep you posted.'

'Please do.' There was another moment, which might have been awkward, but then they filled the gap with a small sort of hug, and Morgana promised she'd be in touch and disappeared out into the night again.

'Very cool.' Gid was still looking at the door. 'Very cool. I always liked her – I just couldn't figure out what had happened over the last few months. She changed – but I hoped she was still there, underneath. I did *kinda* like her.' He grinned at the door.

'Well, now you know. Gid …' Her stomach spun again like a tumble dryer had taken up residence in there. 'How am I going to get to Skye?'

'Hire car?' He shrugged his shoulders and looked down at her, smiling in her direction now. 'If you're happy with that, then let me sort that out for you. We can get something straight away. Pay for an extra day, and you can be away before dawn tomorrow. I know you won't want to wait too long, pointless me telling you to wait until a sensible time, eh? I haven't spent any of that peppercorn rent you gave me for the sofa. I knew this would happen, so I've got it all set aside for your train fare or hire car or whatever. But I think, given the time of year, a car would be best. It might be a struggle to get tickets for anything else. You get yourself packed. And I think tomorrow, I'll take some of your lino prints into the mysticism shop. They'll be good marketing tools for our tattoos, especially if we can convince Zara to have a photo taken once hers is complete.' He grinned that cheeky grin that was so Gid. 'It means, of course, I need to do a trip to Celtic Heart and see the new custodian of the goods.'

'Good luck, Gid,' Ivy said warmly. 'You deserve it. And thank you for everything over these last few months. I really mean it. And a hire car is fine.' She felt laughter and relief bubbling up inside her. Christmas was looking better and better.

'I knew you'd go back,' Gideon said suddenly, startling her. 'That's why I didn't encourage you to try and rent a new place. I knew you'd only be a temporary adornment to my humble abode. You don't belong here, my love. You belong up there.' He pointed in what may have been a northerly direction.

'Where? At the North Pole? With Santa Claus?' She tried to make a joke, because if she didn't, she might just teeter away from laughter, hit the "hysterics" button and start weeping with gratitude, embarrassing herself in front of her friend.

'No. In Skye. With Zac Fallon.'

It sounded so strange for someone to say that – to verbalise what she had suspected for a while, but hadn't wanted to say it out loud. Just in case.

It sounded strange. But also true. And she liked the idea very much indeed.

Chapter Twenty-Two

Ivy left at a ridiculously early hour. Fortunately, she had packed everything the night before, and had, surprisingly, managed to sleep. The temperature had risen above freezing in the night and she hadn't been defeated by icy morning roads. The shiny hire car was parked outside, her luggage was loaded in the back and she just had to drive.

She hoped and prayed the Christmas miracles were still coming her way and also crossed her fingers there would be no snow until she actually got onto Skye. Then maybe, just maybe, she could handle it.

It was the twenty-third of December, Christmas Eve's Eve. She had tried and tried to call Zac numerous times the previous night, and had kept trying at various rest stops on her journey. She wanted to try and tell him she was on her way. She wanted to be there for Christmas Eve. She wanted to have as much of Christmas as possible on the Isle of Skye with the man she now realised she loved and didn't want to live apart from.

She went hot and cold all over. What if he didn't feel the same, though?

The hot-ness and cold-ness were exacerbated by the fact she still couldn't get in touch with him. His mobile was out of service, and even the phone line to his shop and home were just ringing out.

In desperation, from a service station in the Lake District, she rang Angel. It was realistically too late to start second-guessing herself, but she needed some sort of validation.

'It's about time one of you made that decision!' Angel said, amusement in her voice. 'Thank God and all the Christmas angels for it! And me, yes, I am also a Christmas Angel, as I have already told him what he needed to do. I told him he was being silly. He admitted himself he was an eejit, and we know Zac doesn't admit that easily. Ivy, I'm *so* glad you are sensible. But, to answer your question, I can't catch him today either. I don't know if the phone lines are out. I got a text to say he was home, and then I tried to call and we got cut off. It happens up there. And here, at Taigh Fallon. But not so much. It's bad if our WiFi goes off, as Kyle's a bit stuck for work, but it doesn't last long, thankfully.'

'I don't know if sensible is what I'd call it,' said Ivy, thinking of the long journey she still had ahead of her up north, with the possibility of snow. 'But I guess I just have to do it.'

'Do it,' Angel said warmly. 'Do you want me to keep trying to ring him for you?'

'You'd better.' Ivy sighed. 'I don't want to go all the way up there and be chased away.'

'You won't be. But just in case, I'll put both of my sisters on notice, as well as Uncle Donald and Uncle Anthony, and if you change your mind you've got three places at least to call into if you head back. My uncles are peaches, they really are. They'd love to look after you if you needed it. Everyone's coming to us, but not for a day or so, so you'll be sure of a welcome.'

'Thank you. You really are a Christmas Angel aren't you?' Ivy grinned into the phone, feeling inordinately grateful that she had Angel and Angel's sisters and yes, even Angel's uncles, in her life. It made it all seem *possible*.

'Dark Angel maybe,' Angel said with a chuckle. 'That's what Kyle would tell you anyway.'

Ivy laughed. But now she knew she had to stop talking about it, and had to make that possibility of having Christmas on the Isle of Skye with Zac a reality. She took a deep breath, said her farewells to Angel and started the car back up.

He'd arrived back on the Island the day before, and, as luck would have it, the phone lines were still out. There had been flurries all day, and snow was piling up on the side of the roads. Judith was grumbling about customers and dogs and various combinations of customers and dogs, but Zac was refusing to engage. He just mumbled something soothing to her and found solace in his workshop.

He picked up a Celtic knot brooch in the shape of a heart, one of Ivy's that he had never put on general sale, and turned it over and over in his hands. He had handed her the asking price, pretending it had come from a customer and hidden it in his drawer in the workbench ever since. It was maybe a silly little thing to do, but when he needed to feel close to her, he opened the drawer up and put it on the workbench next to him.

It had been constantly on his workbench since April.

'Bloody hell!' He put the brooch down and angrily got his tools out to start on a pair of earrings. 'Boxing Day,' he muttered. 'Boxing Day, I'm going bloody back.' He would have gone there now, but what was the point of ruining everyone's Christmas? She'd be all loved up with her new fiancé, and he'd be there third-wheeling like a pro.

He picked up his phone for the umpteenth time and swore again. There was still no service. He'd had no word from Ivy about her no doubt joyous news, and he couldn't even call

Angel to see if she'd heard from her. Winter weather on the Island sucked sometimes, it really did.

'*Channel your Edgar-ness*,' Angel had told him. Why, though? Why on earth would anyone want an Edgar? He was definitely more Edgar than Heathcliff, he knew that. But passion was something he *did* have. He honestly did have it, but it was buried deep, like a slow-burning flame. Once someone had Zac's heart, they had it forever. Whether, as he had told Ivy, it was Angel who had a special little piece of it in the close bond of friendship they shared; or whether it was the huge part he would lay down happily in front of Ivy if she should be free. Even if she wasn't, he decided he shouldn't give up.

Then he felt like a really bad person, because he was honourable as well, and far be it for him to break up a relationship. Especially if Ivy was happy in it.

Circles. He was going around in circles again.

Okay, so maybe he wouldn't go back Boxing Day. He would have to plan it carefully, discover how the land really lay with Gid, and then decide. And he would back off if he had to. Wasn't that what the remarkable Edgar had done? Allowed Catherine to love Heathcliff quite freely, and lurked in the background of Thrushcross Grange like the good egg he was, just waiting for her to drop Heathcliff like a lump of hot coal? Just hoping that she would somehow forget her other life and love him back.

Zac was fed up of being a good egg, though. And Edgar never truly had Cathy Earnshaw's heart, did he?

However, Cathy was high maintenance. Ivy was easy-going, loving and happy. She was ideal. The absolutely ideal person. And she was in Glastonbury and he was up here.

His bad mood wasn't getting any better, and he wondered if he had a wee bit of the scowly Heathcliff about him anyway?

The irritating, annoying and hopeless thoughts kept him company all afternoon. On auto-pilot, he smiled at his customers, consciously tried to relax his face so he looked less like he ate puppies for breakfast, checked his phone roughly a hundred times more, and swore he felt his heart turning to lead as heavy as the snow showers that they were forecasted well into the evening here.

Some Christmas Eve's Eve this was turning out to be.

Perhaps he'd put the damn Christmas tree up in his croft and sort those lights out on the one Angel had meddled with on the ruined croft. It would take his mind off other things, at least …

Maybe he shouldn't wait until Boxing Day?

He still had a day or so to go back to her.

Stop being daft, Zac! Just stop it!

Aye. Circles. Lots of circles. It felt like he was trapped in the worst sort of holly wreath ever.

He'd go and sort Angel's tree out. At least by doing that, he was well away from any troublesome memories of Ivy – and the cold winter wind might just take his mind off a warm hand, held safely in his, in a snowy Glastonbury.

Chapter Twenty-Three

There were a couple of cars parked to the side of the barns and Ivy's stomach turned over as she, finally, pulled the rental car up beside them. It was real. She was *here*. And Zac had customers, which was always good. It was sort of surprising that he was still open – but as he had often said to her "people expect the place to be open, and so I'll be open". It wasn't even four o'clock yet, although she felt she'd spent at least a year in the damn car.

She'd tried not to think about what she'd do if Zac had decided to go away for Christmas after all – she supposed she would be hammering on the door of the nearest pub, and if not exactly pleading an imminent Virgin Birth at least pleading for a bed for the night.

She hadn't even considered if she would be welcome to stay at Zac's – perhaps that "room at the inn" thing would be a "thing" after all? It didn't bear thinking about. She knew Angel would welcome her at Taigh Fallon – but the thought of another huge chunk of time driving back that way made her want to cry. Her impetus had been to get here, to Skye, to Zac, and she had.

Ivy climbed out of the car and stretched, breathing in the pure air and, despite the fact that her legs felt like jelly and her stomach was now turning somersaults, her heart lifted as it always did when she visited this beautiful part of the world. She had an affinity with the sea, and she'd missed it these last few months. Far above her, the skies were clouding in, grey and white, the last vestiges of daylight disappearing behind the Cuillins as the winter sun set.

There was an odd sort of stillness in the air, hanging heavy with the promise of more snow, and a little thrill ran up and down her shoulder blades as the first few damp flakes started to descend from the heavens. She had made it just in time. Judging by the piles on the sides of the road, they'd already had a downfall, and that would explain the phone lines. They were obviously still down. She'd tried again just before she crossed the bridge to the Island, feeling truly sick to the stomach, half hoping he wouldn't answer – then she would just have to keep going and not give up.

Locking the car, she walked up to the tea room and paused at the door. Despite the uncertainty about what might happen within the next few minutes, she smiled as the memories came back to her. Working in here had been the happiest time of her life – and that didn't seem to be an odd thing to admit at all. Not here, not back on her – on *their* – very special territory.

'We're closing.' A woman barked the sentence out at her, as she seemingly appeared out of nowhere and flipped the *Open* sign over. Two harried families were apparently in the process of being evicted from the tea room. One woman had a square shape wrapped in a napkin, which was, presumably, the remainder of her snack. Ivy stared at the woman. Judith. This had to be her.

'And Merry Christmas to you too!' Ivy was appalled. She was so appalled, she didn't even qualify her purpose there. Instead, she turned away and ran towards the workshop she knew Zac would be in.

'Zac!' She flung the door open. 'I came back. I came—'

But the room was empty. The tools were neatly put away and the main lights were off. There were some half-finished pieces of jewellery on the bench, but that was typically Zac. He'd leave something and come back to it if it wasn't working for him.

'Zac?' She tried his name again, looking around her wildly, wondering if by any chance he would pop out from under the workbench when he heard her. The sight of his cup, the one she had always brought him his coffee in, all washed and put away on the windowsill where he always kept it at the end of the day upset her more than it really should have done. And the sight of an awfully familiar Celtic knot brooch, just where he sat to do his work, made her stomach turn over.

She remembered the day she'd allegedly sold it – he'd been vague and waved his hand in the direction of the sea. '*Some tourist bought it. They said it was just perfect,*' he'd told her. '*It's a shame. It was my favourite thing in the workshop. Well.*' He'd looked at her and blushed, and it seemed as if he was about to say something else. '*It was my favourite thing, until you walked in.*'

'*Me?*' she'd asked, hardly daring to breathe.

'*Aye.*' Then he turned it all into a joke '*That's my coffee cup and a slice of cake, if I'm not mistaken. They're pretty hard to beat in the favourite stakes.*' Then he'd dipped his head to his work and denied any knowledge of anything else relating to that transaction.

But now she understood. He'd never sold it at all – he'd kept it. 'Oh no!' She spun around and stared at the door, half-expecting that Judith woman to come in after her and wave a butter knife around in the hope of chasing her off the premises. 'Oh, Zac ...'

Ivy felt her mouth turn downwards and her bottom lip begin to tremble. She bit it angrily. If she was going to collapse into a heap of annoyed sobbing, she'd do that well away from Judith and her butter knife.

She was too late after all. He'd perhaps already finished and had asked Judith to lock the doors on her way out. She had done that several times for him herself if he needed to make one of his hated visits to the mainland and had to catch a particular ferry. She swore under her breath and tried to think logically. Well, if she could get those keys from Judith, she could wait at his croft, she supposed – but what if he was away for any length of time? That would be just silly.

This had been a very stupid idea. Very stupid indeed. She took one last look at the window, then saw a twinkling light come on just across the field. It was that old croft Kyle was renovating – the light seemed to be coming from quite high up and she frowned. Moving closer to the window, Ivy saw the illuminated outline of a tree balanced on scaffolding ...

And, even better, a tall, rangy, shadowy figure walking away from the place. Her heart somersaulted and her exhausted energy came back to her in a burst of electricity. She knew exactly who that figure was. He walked the way she'd dreamed of him walking, perfectly at ease in the wild countryside, the mountains black against the grey sky. More snowflakes were falling now, piling up in the corners of the window, covering the ground he walked on.

The ground she was going to cover in as few steps as possible, just as soon as she ran out of his workshop.

Chapter Twenty-Four

The figure appeared around the corner of the workshop; at first, he thought he was dreaming. 'Ivy?' Zac stopped and stared as she hurtled towards him, her arms outstretched. 'Ivy!' He caught her as she threw herself into his arms. 'What on earth? Is it you? Is it *really* you, or have I fallen down a damned rabbit hole, cracked my head and sent myself doolally?'

'No, you're not doolally!' She was half-laughing, half-crying. 'God, I thought I'd missed you, I thought you'd shut up shop. I thought I was too late!'

'You've done a lot of thinking, lassie!' Zac drew her close and squeezed her hard, his eyes closed. This had to be a fleeting visit; he had no right to think she was coming here for any reason beyond popping in to see her old workplace before heading off elsewhere. 'Is Gid with you?' He managed to choke out the man's name. God, perhaps they'd come up in person to share the news of their Solstice engagement?

'Gid? No. He's probably with Morgana, rolling around in ecstasy on his bed now my sofa is vacated. I'm just on my own.'

'On your own? But how are you so calm about it?' Zac was horrified. 'You and him were living together! He proposed to you!'

'Didn't you hear me?' She laughed. 'I just said – I was on his *sofa*. We were living together through sheer *necessity*! And he didn't propose. Whatever Morgana told you was wrong.

I've been trying to call you all day. I wanted you to know I was coming. And I wanted to put you right about Gid. I even called Angel.'

Zac felt his eyes widen as he stared at her. Her hair was being blown about by the harsh north wind, and snowflakes were sprinkled all over by now.

'My phone lines are down,' he said faintly. 'I haven't had any calls or texts for hours now. Ivy! I love this place, but in cases like this – good lord!' He pulled her closer, not wanting to let her go. She wasn't with Gid! She was here. She was on Skye, in his arms …

Her nose was pink and her eyes were bright, and suddenly she laughed. 'Oh my goodness. If you really thought I was with Gid – no wonder you disappeared so quickly. Was that what you meant? About if things were different?'

'Well, what was I supposed to do?' He grinned, then laughed out loud. 'Greet the hairy beast with "hey, I got a wee bit carried away with your girlfriend, I kissed her and held her hand a bit too long on the Solstice celebration. I could have run away with her under my arm, and I really wanted to, by the way. Hope that's okay with you?"'

'Zac! Hairy beast? I thought you were *over* all that? Gid is no more hairy than you, and you *know* that! And honestly, despite what you thought, or what my stupid ramblings *made* you think, he's just a good friend. My version of your Angel. We've never been anything else. Never would be.' She reached up and rumpled his hair, which was, yes, down to his shoulders, now it was wet and bedraggled. It probably wasn't his best look.

And Gid was a friend. Well, it wasn't entirely surprising he'd assumed otherwise – hadn't Morgana implied they were a couple; and hadn't Kyle, all those months ago when he'd first burst into Taigh Fallon in the middle of the night, thought the same about him and Angel to start with? How daft. How daft he was. He'd never learn. Edgar might have let his Cathy go at the first hurdle, but Heathcliff wouldn't.

Zac reached out and caught Ivy's hand, enclosing it in his. 'Your hand's frozen.' Suddenly, the words were difficult to speak. The feel of her cold skin against his, the shivers that were zipping around his scalp as she touched him. 'Ivy McFarlane. What have you done to me?'

'I've come back,' she murmured. Almost imperceptibly, something shifted in the atmosphere. 'And I'm not going to be able to walk away again ... I'm not going to be able to ...' She stumbled over her words and looked down, her cheeks now tinged a brighter pink than her nose. Her hair fell over her face, but Zac caught the fleeting expression there. 'I'm not going to be able to,' she repeated. 'I can't. I don't want to. It was awful, Zac. I never made such a mistake in my life.' The floodgates had apparently opened and the words came tumbling out, all knotted up like so much tinsel tangled in a Christmas tree. 'The shop was awful, and living on Gid's sofa was the absolute worst. I love Glastonbury, I really do, but I never settled. It was all rubbish, everything I told you about it being the best place for me to work. I'd go back to visit like a shot, but I never want to try working there again. There was too much pressure on me. My prints did well, but the customers had to get past Morgana first, and she didn't make things easy for me – so Gid's got the prints in the mysticism shop, because he knows I'm not going back, and Morgana's had a change of heart and is going to sell my stuff online and in the shop. She said she'll look after things until I decide what to do, but I've already decided, and even if you don't want me here—'

Zac put his finger on her lips. 'Shhhh …' Gently, he moved his hand and tilted her head up to face him, hoping those eyes would fix on his and he could drown in her sea-green gaze, troubled as it was at the moment with a million conflicting emotions swirling around. 'Who says I don't want you here? And not going back to Glastonbury is not a big deal. You tried. And you had to do it. Even if I'd fought to keep you here, even if I had stopped you, you'd never have forgiven me when you'd thought about it reasonably. So, shall we agree to disagree about it?'

She half-sobbed, then almost laughed. 'Please. Let's just do that, aye?' Her accent was stronger, he noticed, enhanced by emotion.

He rubbed his thumb gently down her cheek. 'Aye. We'll do that then. And if you *did* go back, Ivy, I'd miss you too much anyway.'

'But how? How would you miss me? Because if it's just a case of having someone help you out here, or look after the place when you're away, or do a bit of work for you to sell in the shop, then a hundred other people, probably more, could do as well as I do …' Her voice started to rise again, then she seemed to stop herself and frowned. 'Perhaps not Judith, though. She's binned your customers, you do know that, don't you?'

Zac smiled and shook his head. 'That's not surprising. And nobody is a patch on you. Judith is simply plugging a gap. Can you help me get someone new?'

'No.' She shook her head. 'I'm coming back, regardless. I like dogs. I like customers. I like you.'

'Just like?' He was teasing her.

'No. Maybe more than like.'

'I more than like you too, Ivy McFarlane. And I can't imagine *not* having you here.' He shook his head, knowing it was true. Suddenly serious, he took her face in his hands again. 'Ivy. I want you with me. Properly. I don't know how I've existed since April. I really don't.'

She stared up at him, her eyes widening, her mouth a little surprised "o". It was too much to resist.

He leaned down and kissed her, right on the little "o".

'Properly,' he repeated, just so she was sure.

Ivy stared at him, then the most perfect smile broke out across her face. 'Tell me you're not going all Heathcliff on me? All "I cannot live without my soul".' She stared up at him, shaking her head, amused. 'And there's you always saying you don't get all that rubbish!' Then, happily for Zac, she flung her arms around him, holding him tight, butting her head into the crook of his shoulder as if it belonged there. As if she wanted to do it forever more. 'I think you *do* get it, you really do. Oh God, this could have gone either way. I'm so pleased I came here, I'm so very, very pleased.'

Zac closed his eyes briefly, breathing out a sigh of relief and squeezed her just as tightly, feeling her strong back and her slim body beneath his hands. He buried his face in her hair and kissed the unruly curls, covered now with snowflakes. Ivy was his missing piece. There seemed to have been an Ivy-shaped hole in his life for as long as he could remember. Now he felt complete.

He smiled against her hair and pulled away, ever so slightly, remembering something. 'You know what Angel said, last time she was up here?' Ivy shook her head, her eyes searching his with so many unanswered questions – so many things they needed to settle about the future, their future, and how they could start it properly. 'Angel told me about that Christmas tree,' he continued. 'The one just over there, on the roof of the croft. I've just spent half an hour sorting the fairy lights out on it.' Taking hold of her around the waist, he turned her around so she was facing the croft, the jagged Cuillins behind it, a covering of white on them now and white as far as the eyes could see on the moors beyond Zac's land. 'Angel suggested something else it needed. And I knew it myself. Knew it here. In my heart.' He pressed her hand to his chest. 'I spent even longer winding an ivy garland around that damn Christmas tree. Just because I absolutely needed it. The tree wasn't complete – not until you came. Nothing was complete. Because I needed ivy, you see. I needed ivy on the tree, and I need you – I need Ivy in my life. And do you know what I was going to do? On Boxing Day?'

Ivy turned to face him. 'No?'

'I was coming back down.'

'Really? Via Bristol? Via your cousins?'

'Yes, *really* coming back. But not via Bristol. I haven't got any family in Bristol. I came via Whitby the first time – a bit more of a diversion, but *entirely* worth it.' He smiled at her stunned expression as realisation dawned. 'I had talked myself back into it, and I was going to drive back down and try to persuade you to come back with me. Again. And I would have kept going back, and finding excuse after excuse to do so – just to see you. Which is maybe a wee bit weird, but I don't want to be without you. Without—' his smile grew wider '—my soul. You know how it goes.'

Ivy stood on tiptoe. She kissed him gently and he pulled

her closer again. He wished he could pull her closer still – but not here, not on the wild, wintry moors. That would come later, in the warm croft when they were exactly where they needed to be this Christmas Eve's Eve and all the days of Christmas beyond, and all the Christmases ahead. And that was in each other's arms.

'You've got her,' Ivy said. 'You've got your soul. And she's not going anywhere.'

'So, you'll bide a wee while then? Maybe until Christmas Day?' He smiled down at her, feeling the happiest he had ever felt in his life. 'There's a ceilidh on later tonight at the local. They might just do a Hooligan's Jig, if you fancy it again. Because by the looks of things, you'll probably be snowed in here anyway.' The snow was falling thicker and faster, covering their footprints, as if they'd never been anywhere else at all.

'I'll stay forever. If you'll have me?'

'I will.'

'I'll have you too.'

'Good. Our souls are the same, you know? Yours and mine.'

'I know, Zac. I know.'

And, as more fresh snow swept in from the mountains and blurred the coloured lights on the Christmas tree, and their cold lips met in another kiss, they both knew that forever wouldn't be long enough.

Thank You

Thank you so much for reading, and hopefully enjoying, *Christmas on the Isle of Skye*. I trust you agree that Zac and Ivy made the right decision in the end!

However, authors also need to know they are doing the right thing, and keeping our readers happy is a huge part of the job. So, it would be wonderful if you could find a moment just to write a quick review on the website where you purchased the book to let me know that you enjoyed it. Thank you once again, and do feel free to contact me at any time on Facebook, Twitter, through my website or through my lovely publishers Choc Lit.

Thanks again, and much love to you all,

Kirsty

xx

About the Author

Kirsty Ferry is from the North East of England and lives there with her husband and son. She won the English Heritage/Belsay Hall National Creative Writing competition in 2009 and has had articles and short stories published in various magazines. Her work also appears in several anthologies, incorporating such diverse themes as vampires, crime, angels and more.

Kirsty loves writing ghostly mysteries and interweaving fact and fiction. The research is almost as much fun as writing the book itself, and if she can add a wonderful setting and a dollop of history, that's even better. Her day job involves sharing a building with an eclectic collection of ghosts, which can often prove rather interesting.

For more information on Kirsty visit:
www.twitter.com/kirsty_ferry
https://www.facebook.com/kirsty.ferry.author/

More Choc Lit

From Kirsty Ferry

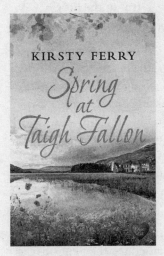

Spring at Taigh Fallon

From old secrets come new beginnings ...

When Angel Tempest finds out that her best friend Zac has inherited a Scottish mansion, Taigh Fallon, from his great aunt, she immediately offers to go and visit it with him. It will mean closing up her jet jewellery shop in Whitby for a few days but the prospect of a spring trip to the Scottish Highlands is too tempting.

Then Kyle, Zac's estranged and slightly grumpy Canadian cousin, unexpectedly turns up at Taigh Fallon, and events take a strange turn as the long-kept secrets of the old house begin to reveal themselves ...

Jessie's Little Bookshop by the Sea

Take a trip to the little bookshop by the sea …

Jessie Tempest has two main interests: reading books and selling books. Her little bookshop in the seaside town of Staithes is a cosy hideaway from the chilly Yorkshire wind, but it's also Jessie's sanctuary from the outside world.

When writer Miles Fareham and his son Elijah arrive to stay in the holiday apartment above the shop, it's a test for Jessie who has always felt clueless when it comes to kids. But as she learns the story of the single father and the inquisitive eight-year-old, Jessie realises that first impressions aren't always the right ones – and, of course, you can never judge a book by its cover!

Summer at Carrick Park

A summer wedding, fifty cupcakes and a man she thought she would never see again …

When Joel Leicester walks into the hotel where Rosa Tempest works, she can't believe her bad luck. Out of all the hotels in all of North Yorkshire, the man who broke her heart would have to walk into Carrick Park!

The last time Rosa saw Joel it was after a whirlwind holiday when they'd been greeted at his flat by a woman claiming to be his fiancée. Rosa never stuck around to hear Joel's side of the story but now, six years later on, Fate has another trick up its sleeve as a potentially disastrous summer wedding at Carrick Park can only be saved by Joel and Rosa working together …

Visit www.choc-lit.com for details.

The Schubert Series

A series of quirky romcoms set in Edinburgh and featuring a big black cat called Schubert!

Every Witch Way – Book 1

A Christmas Secret – Book 2

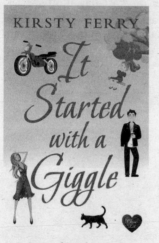

It Started With a Giggle
– Book 3

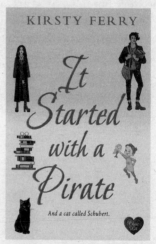

It Started With a Pirate
– Book 4

The Cornish Secrets Series

A charming collection of time-slip romances set in the same Cornish arts centre.

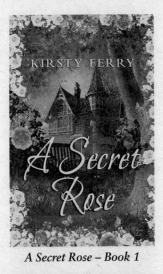

A Secret Rose – Book 1

Lily's Secret – Book 2

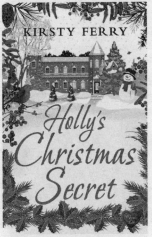

Holly's Christmas Secret – Book 3

Summer's Secret Marigold – Book 4

The Hartsford Mysteries

A series of atmospheric time-slip romances, all set in the same beautiful mansion house in Suffolk.

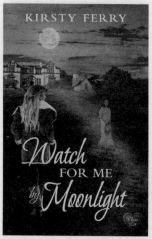

Watch for Me by Moonlight – Book 1

Watch for Me by Candlelight – Book 2

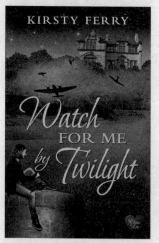

Watch for Me by Twilight – Book 3

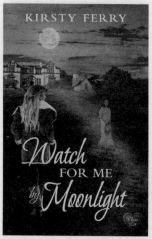

Watch for Me at Christmas – Book 4

The Rossetti Mysteries

*A series of compelling time-slip romances set
in the art world in Yorkshire and London.*

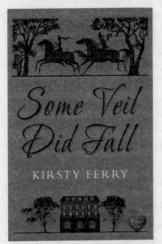

**Some Veil Did Fall
– Book 1**

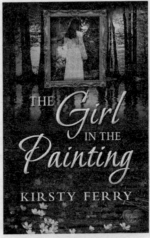

**The Girl in the Painting
– Book 2**

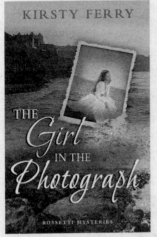

**The Girl in the Photograph
– Book 3**

**A Little Bit of Christmas
Magic – Book 4**

Visit www.choc-lit.com for more details.

Introducing Choc Lit

We're an independent publisher creating
a delicious selection of fiction.
Where heroes are like chocolate – irresistible!
Quality stories with a romance at the heart.

See our selection here:
www.choc-lit.com

We'd love to hear how you enjoyed *Christmas on the
Isle of Skye*. Please visit **www.choc-lit.com** and give your
feedback or leave a review where you purchased this novel.

Choc Lit novels are selected by genuine readers like yourself.
We only publish stories our Choc Lit Tasting Panel want to
see in print. Our reviews and awards speak for themselves.

Could you be a Star Selector and join our Tasting Panel?
Would you like to play a role in choosing which novels
we decide to publish? Do you enjoy reading women's
fiction? Then you could be perfect for our Tasting Panel.

Visit here for more details…
www.choc-lit.com/join-the-choc-lit-tasting-panel

Keep in touch:
Sign up for our monthly newsletter Spread for all the latest
news and offers: www.spread.choc-lit.com. Follow us
on Twitter: @ChocLituk and Facebook: Choc Lit.

Where heroes are like chocolate – irresistible!